The Eyes of Death

Book III of The Blades of Dawn

by Vasilis Petrovic

ISBN: 978-960-93-9519-9

Revised edition, 2025

Cover Illustration: Korey Barton
https://www.facebook.com/KoreyBarton.Art

Cover Design: Thanos Petrovic
http://petrovicnasos.wixsite.com/athanasios-petrovits

Here you can find links to my books as well as free RPG accessories and adventures:
https://petrovicvasilis.wixsite.com/age-of-thunder

If I've moved on from Wix, you can find info on where I'm currently based in the 'Age of Thunder' Discord server,
https://discord.gg/rBgexVTAyz

Drop me a line regarding this book at petrovic.vasilis@gmail.com

My Amazon Author Central page,
https://www.amazon.com/author/vasilispetrovic

If you're so inclined, you can buy me a cold Beer – I'm always thirsty!
https://www.buymeacoffee.com/cimmerian

Dedicated to Dimitris, Efthimis, Thanasis and all the other adventurers who have been members of the Shadows of the Blade

Lastly and always, dedicated to Robert E. Howard who came with pen in hand to tread the pages of fantasy with a Cimmerian's feats

Table of Contents

The events of this book take place during the year 128 DT (after the Day of Thunder,) before the Olympic Games opened to mortals. This period marks the first steps of the newborn dorian kingdoms on the face of Gaea (also called Earth.) It is a time of change, characterized by strife and war between the dorians and their many enemies. In time, the entire second century of the Age of Thunder will come to be called the Red Years.

In this period, life is a harsh experience. Violence is often the only way to keep your freedom and your dignity and the rule of law is a rare thing. The arts and the crafts are taught again by the Gods to chosen mortals who in turn teach others and civilization is built brick by brick on the ruins left by the people of past ages.

The Gods (also called Dodecatheon) have returned to the world and they rule from their seat of power on Mount Olympos. Zeus is the King of the Dodecatheon and the kings of the dorian realms rule in his name. The secrets of mysticism are discovered anew but the process is slow and perilous because the Orphic texts are rediscovered and often rewritten and the knowledge of astral archetypes and quintessential constructs unravels the fragile mortality of those mystics who are not strong enough to endure the power of magic. Priests are rare and are commonly called wise or holy and they wield but a fraction of the power that they'll come to hold in more civilized eras. The gift of healing is possessed by only a few and they are the holiest of all and they're called Hieroi.

The spawn of the Dark Host, the despised followers of the Adversary, elder beasts that bear only hatred for mortals and monsters of every size and shape, lay equal claim to the land, the wind and the water as do the danaoi, the chalyvoi, the sylfaen, the centaurs and all the other human races. The Firstborn have just been dethroned from supremacy over the Earth by the Olympians but they are still here. Dragons have been here since the beginning and they will always be here.

The building of civilization begins by teaching the children and so every child learns to read and write, to play music and to sing. Moreover, children are taught some of the secrets of numbers and of the holy shapes - the triangle, the circle and the square. But a child's education begins with the simple truth about the world, imparted when it is old enough to understand it. This truth is measured by only a few words but it forces the child to turn the page and leave innocence behind.

The Muses whisper to us, mortals, in song and in dream and in the voices of leaf and water and tell us of how things were in the Ages of Myth. From them we know of our past, of the Cosmogony and the Titanomachy and all the other ages, before this one. But those ages are gone, all the grand works of mortals are dust and the wonders we had achieved are but faded memories of ancient glories.

What matters now is that we win the war that rages on the Earth and in the Heavens. This Age of Thunder, born in cataclysmic fury is what we have and what we are. What we do now will determine whether another age will succeed the thunder or whether the Cosmos will be surrendered to the empty darkness.

This, my child, is your world.

Chapter 1. The Quest

Year 129 DT, month of the Eagle.
Earthembar Mountains, the Temple of Glass.

The gigantic gates of the temple, that were as tall as a three-story building, closed behind Alopex and Silidora with a resounding crash that made the ground tremble and their ears hurt. Ordinarily, human petitioners would depart from the normal-sized door inset in one of the obsidian gates. However, the Seeress of Glass had ordered that the temple gates be opened for their departure, as a sign of honour for those who embark on a quest ordained by the temple. A string of profanities was uttered by Alopex that went unheard because he, Silidora and the chalyvoi were deafened by the closing of the gates. The youngest of the brother-kings of Chalkaea did not feel particularly honoured.

"...amn her eyes, ouch, I think my ears are bleeding." Alopex was hunched over and had his hands over his ears. His slim crown, a plain copper circlet with a small ruby inlaid at the front, had fallen off his head. He was a handsome man of straw-blond hair and light-blue eyes, tall and well-built. He wore a plain, woolen chiton, a gold-stitched chlamys over that and the winter cloak called himation. Well-worn sandals on his feet and a wide, leather waistbelt completed his kingly appearance. Four long knives were sheathed on the belt itself, the sheaths of two double-bladed daggers hung from it and two more knives were in calf-sheaths.

"Stop whining, Alopex. You danaoi are so sensitive, sometimes." Silidora said.

She was a sylfaea of rare beauty; she had short hair of the dark green colour of an unlighted leaf or black with a green sheen, it was difficult to tell. Her eyes were amber jewels and her skin was smooth and milk-white that glistened under direct sunlight. She cut a striking figure in her black chiton, hard-soled sandals, body-sculpted breastplate and backplate of heavy, promethean steel with matching vambraces and greaves as well as a miter and wings for protection of her groin and upper legs. A linen chlamys was fastened over her left shoulder with a silver clasp in the shape of a dolphin. Her leaf-shaped sword, a distinctive sylfan blade, was sheathed and hung from her waistbelt along with a quiver of white-fletched arrows. She had her long bow in hand. She was too lightly dressed for the cold and snow of the mountain because she had no need for warmer clothing. It was her sylfan birthright to endure extremes of heat and cold that would discomfit or even kill other dorians.

Alopex straightened and assumed a dignified posture, a grimace of exasperation on his face.

"A king never whines, Silidora. Every word he says is a pearl of wisdom. You would do well to remember that. Now, stop mumbling and pick up my crown." He said and indicated the fallen circlet.

"The Gods saw fit to give you hands Alopex, pick it up yourself." Silidora retorted.

The familiarity implied by their verbal sparring was plain to see but Nargi was as blind to it as a mole and so he thought that the two talls were moments away from a fight. He was the youngest of the chalyvoi who were to lead the questors to their city and the shortest of them all, he didn't reach over a meter and thirty. There were eight chalyvoi in all, led by the white-haired elder, Chryssa Goldheart. They wore an assortment of armours, mostly leather breastplates, studded with bronze disks and most carried gate shields - the distinctive orthogonal shields of the tunnel-fighter. They favoured their traditional weapons - picks and hammers - and a few also carried crossbows.

Nargi picked up the circlet and examined the poorly-made thing with a sour face. He tightened two of the prongs that held the ruby in place with his knife and handed it to Alopex. Nargi wanted to tell the king that the ruby was in fact a garnet of low value but he was too shy. He had the natural respect for authority of every decent chalyvos and was somewhat awed by the presence of a king, even one as unlikely as Alopex.

"Thank you my friend." Alopex told Nargi and examined the crown himself. "Rather poor isn't it?" He asked and Nargi nodded.

Alopex rummaged in his sack, brought out a similar crown and put it upon his brow. Although the new crown was also a slim circlet, with an inset, faceted ruby, it was nothing like the other one. One could say that the difference was that of a river pebble compared to a well-cut gem. Both were rocks but they were nothing alike. Nargi's mouth hung open when he saw the exquisite workmanship, the minute detail of etch-work and the perfect clarity and deep tone of the huge ruby. That was indeed a crown fit for a king. Alopex winked to the young chalyvos.

"It wouldn't do for the seeress to think that I'm a rich king - she'd ask for more wealth than my poor kingdom can afford. The Gods know our offerings were kingly enough as it is." The brother-king said and turned to the eldest of the chalyvoi. "Chryssa Goldheart, I commend you. Your people have proper respect for a king."

The elderly chalyvaea only nodded at the remark. Silidora snorted at the comment but gave the danaos no more attention. She kept looking all around her and up at the clouded sky while walking slowly down the only path that led away from the temple, a path whose boundaries were marked by chiseled blocks of volcanic glass. It was aptly named the 'Path of Glass.'

Silidora enjoyed the wind on her skin, the sight of the open sky, the sounds of birds and the fragrance of the first flowers of spring. One could tell these things just by looking at her or so young Nargi assured me when he told me the story. He was quite smitten with her.

Alopex faced the gates, assumed what he considered to be a kingly pose - legs apart, hands on his waist, his head held high - and shouted at the top of his lungs, *"I know that you can hear me guardian of the gate. Come out fellow and pay homage to the heroes who go on a quest at the bidding of the seeress."*

No one appeared to pay him homage.

"The petraean giant is merged with the stone, King Alopex, ready to challenge new arrivals. I don't think that he's going to emerge for those leaving the temple," Chryssa said in a neutral voice.

"Just as I thought; he only knows how to intimidate travelers who arrive to seek an oracle, but knows not how to honour them or apologize for his behaviour. We are Dorians, we are the People of the Spear, so named by the Olympians when we battled Titans and Gigantes together in the Titanomachy. You are wise to remain hidden in our presence, giant."

Silence followed the angry words of Alopex. Nargi's mouth hung open, Chryssa had a grim expression and Silidora stared daggers at Alopex and had her hand on her blade's grip. Five heartbeats passed, then five more and the giant still hadn't emerged.

Silidora broke the silence. "I think that we tarried enough here. I for one, had enough of being virtually locked up in the temple, no matter how high the ceilings and how large the spaces inside and would prefer to get going as soon as possible. The Worldmother never stands still and neither should we."

"That is so. We waste good light and we've far to go." Chryssa's words galvanized the rest of the chalyvoi who wanted to be away from there and fast, lest the petraean's anger was belatedly awakened.

"Very well, let's be off. Lead the way, Chryssa Goldheart." Alopex commanded.

He was unconcerned about the danger and his own anger had gone as swiftly as it had come - his mood swings were bewildering for a stout chalyvos. He'd be young by chalyvan reckoning but he'd reached his middle age as danaoi counted time, as he'd seen forty winters. Even so, maturity seemed to have escaped him. He was a young king who thought too much of himself and of giving orders. Frivolity is often said to be a danaan trait. The constant issuing of orders must be a trait of danaan kings too, I would think. It's true that neither I, nor any of the chalyvoi of Chryssa's company had ever met another danaan king and so, Alopex set the measure for all of them. None of us was impressed, at first. As it was, my people were all too eager to be on their way and didn't disparage Alopex's orders. He was after all, a king and sent on a quest, along with Silidora Windwhisper of Mereandil Wood, to eliminate the greatest threat that our polis had known in its two hundred years. The least we could do was give him the respect due his crown.

The travelers didn't stay on the path of glass for long. The path led north and then west and Glistenwall Hold was located in the land south of the twin mountains. There was no path leading to that land that had no proper name and was simply called the Midlands. Therefore, the company had to make their own way down the mountain. Chryssa's party had already made the journey once, in colder weather and deeper snow and for some of them this wasn't even the first time that they had visited the temple. The talls, as we chalyvoi call danaoi and sylfaen, hadn't been on the mountains before but they had no trouble with the journey. They were people used to hardship and to life on the road.

The initial enthusiasm born of leaving the temple where the chalyvoi had spent long weeks awaiting the pleasure of the seeress, wore out quickly. Contrary to the talls, the chalyvoi preferred enclosed spaces and a sky of stone over their heads. Alopex and Silidora were always ranging ahead of the slower-moving chalyvoi. Their impatience and their constant urging to the company to move faster exasperated my short-legged kin. There was nothing to be done however, other than plodding slowly and carefully through the snow that carpeted the upper slopes of Southembar mountain.

Alopex and Nargi had carried all the waterskins, to fill them from the runoff of melting ice that had made a small stream near their camping site.

"How many days to reach your polis do you figure?" Alopex asked the young chalyvos.

Nargi sighed. It seemed that all that interested the two talls was the swift end of the journey that had only just began.

"We are used to the impatience of talls but you and your companion seem to walk on hot coals instead of deep snow. The others jest that you'd rather fly than walk and even then you'd surely wish for larger wings!" Nargi said with some exasperation.

He'd overcome his shyness by the end of the first day and he was eager to talk to the king, even if it was about the annoying habits of talls.

"I knew it! I was certain that you were laughing at us." Alopex smiled as he said that, to show that he thought nothing of it. "I regret that I don't speak your language. I never had much interest in learning the languages of the other dorian races but I have come to see the merit in it. I wonder why there is no road that leads to the lowlands. After all, that land is claimed by the giants of Krimasand. One would think that the king of Krimasand would want to link his kingdom to the fiefdoms of giants in the Earthembars and especially to the Temple of Glass." Alopex mused aloud.

His mind flitted from one topic to the next faster than a butterfly beat its wings but Nargi had gotten used to this as well.

"The giants of Krimasand aren't on good terms with those of the Earthembars. Some ancient feud, although no dorian of the Hold or of the surrounding land really knows why. So, no road was built and no giants live in the lowlands south of the mountain. I wouldn't have it any other way." Nargi answered and then eyed the king and asked the question that had been on his mind since the morning. "Your crown, it's of chalyvan make, isn't it?"

"Yes, friend Nargi, it was given to me as a gift by the great thane of Dorgobek, Barunn Redcoal himself. My brother has the same one but with a purple sapphire."

"Really?" Asked Nargi, wide-eyed and eager to hear more of the doings of kings. "Why did he make them for you? Did you do something for the great thane? Does that make you subservient kings under Dorgobeks crown? What happened to Chalkaea's last king? Why isn't your brother here with you?"

"Too many questions and each of those answers are long stories in and of themselves. The answer to the last one is obvious though, someone must take care of the kingdom in my absence. Glaucos is the strategos of the Chalkaean Alliance as well as a king, his place is there and mine is here. As for the last king, Durnan Wheelcopper fell in battle against oroks...and worse."

There was a short pause after this and Nargi waited for more. However, Alopex had a faraway look and wasn't going to elaborate on the circumstances of his and his brother's crowning. After a while, when they were nearly done with filling the skins, Nargi dared to ask one more question that was on his mind.

"I was wondering King Alopex, does the Maiden of Mereandil owe you fealty?"

Alopex chuckled as he stoppered the last skin. "Not her. I tried to draft her in my royal guard but she refused."

Nargi was inordinately pleased at Alopex's reply. The king noticed that and asked, "You just won a bet, didn't you?"

Nargi's face reddened and he smiled sheepishly. "I did. Byrrna was of the opinion that a king never travels alone, therefore Silidora must be your personal guard and a loyal subject, despite the fact that she was rude to you this morning as well as every time that someone met both of you in the temple, during your stay. It's certainly strange that a king travels alone but I said that a king would be a fitting companion for the Maiden of Mereandil and not the other way around."

"What? Why would you think that?" Alopex asked with a bit more amusement than outrage.

"Well, it's just that...no one's even heard of you and your brother...and your kingdom is small and poor and your crown is so small and plain - but the new one is much better - and everyone knows and respects the Maiden..." Nargi stammered his reply and then inwardly cursed himself for a haybrained fool. That wasn't a decent thing to say to a king. He stammered an apology.

Fortunately, Alopex was more amused than insulted. "Well, you can say that I'm a stranger to this land and that's a long story as well. Do me a favour and don't tell Silidora that a king would be a fitting companion for her. It might go to her head."

Nargi nodded his agreement vigorously. They had finished their work, yet they remained by the stream. Alopex was watchful of their surroundings, as if he was expecting something. Nargi didn't mind and waited with him. He decided to ask a few more questions - he really was full of them.

"Why do you travel alone really? Shouldn't you have guards with you?"

"My kingdom is indeed small and poor and we are at war. I asked no one to accompany me and the truth is there was no one to spare. However, the captain of the royal guard did volunteer to accompany me." Alopex answered while scanning their surroundings.

"Really? What happened to him?"

"He was denied entrance to the temple by the guard at the gate and had to stay outside while Silidora and I were guests of the seeress of glass. I thought that he'd be here by now *but he is an inordinately shy man and so many chalyvoi must have intimidated him.*" Alopex spoke too loudly as if he wanted someone to hear him, which was strange since they were alone or so Nargi thought.

Alopex had scarcely finished his last sentence when the youth heard footsteps in the snow and the swish of branches behind them. He threw down the flasks he'd been holding, took his warhammer out of his belt loop and held it with both hands as he turned. Alopex turned with arms spread and smiled at the newcomer. A man was coming towards them, covered in a heavy, woolen and dirty himation and a hooded cloak of oiled leather. The hood was pulled low over his face. He plowed through the snow with hard-soled sandals. His silver hands gleamed in the last rays of the sun. Alopex put an arm around the chalyvos' shoulder.

"Nargi Alewood, meet the captain of my royal guard, Malus Argent."

Nargi relaxed, replaced his warhammer in his belt loop and looked at the newcomer with wide, curious eyes. The man named Malus came to stand before them and pulled back his hood, revealing a face of perfect proportions, totally devoid of hair and coated with silver paint, just like his hands (or so it seemed at first examination). His eyes were the striking silver-gray of rainclouds. Alopex and Malus clasped each other's left forearm in the warrior's salute and placed their free hands on each other's shoulders. An easy smile and a look of brotherly affection was on both their faces. They spoke no words of greeting. Then Malus greeted Nargi by shaking hands with him. Malus' hand was cold and too hard to be flesh; it was a hand that belonged to a statue, if statues could move and talk that is. The truth dawned on Nargi that he had before him a man of silver, not a dorian of flesh and blood. The lad was so surprised that he was struck speechless and had no questions for a change.

After a modest meal of dried apples and salted meat with raisins and olives on the side and a cup of wine to wash it down, the chalyvoi settled and took out their pipes. The smokeweed bag passed from one hand to the other and each took out a pinch of the cut and dried leaves to stuff into their pipes. The pipes were lighted with sticks from the fire, the aromatic smoke was inhaled, the pipes relighted until the weed burned well and the chalyvoi began puffing contentedly.

That first night they had taken shelter in a large cave, a spot that was regularly used in their treks on the mountain. There were pitons driven into the stone at the ceiling and from them hung a large sheet of canvas to cover the entrance and keep out some of the wind and the cold. They'd found dry firewood, already piled inside the cave from when they had last been here, on their way to the temple. They'd already gathered more wood to replace the one they'd use for the fire that night. The men had urinated around the entrance of the cave so that the smell would perhaps keep away bears and other beasts.

Alopex brought out a pipe as well, plain but well-made and he was included in the sharing of the smokeweed with a grunt by sour-faced Byrrna who handed him the bag. She had lost money and eyed him and Silidora with suspicion all night, ready to pick up on anything that betrayed the sylfaea as his subject. The only ones not smoking were Silidora and Malus and the cave soon filled with a sweet-smelling haze. The silence stretched. The chalyvoi were people of few words around strangers and it took them some time to get comfortable with new acquaintances. One day was barely enough. During their stay in the temple, the two groups hadn't encountered each other often, since they were assigned to different sections of the temple and were discouraged from roaming. Also, those talls weren't exactly easy to get comfortable with. They were both impatient and not at all happy with the quest they'd been given, that much was obvious. Malus was a surprise and a mystery to all and although they were too polite to talk about him in his presence, all chalyvoi stole looks of curiosity and wonder at the man of silver.

Alopex and Silidora were lost in their own thoughts and in no mood for conversation. Silidora gazed at the play of the crackling flames with a faraway look. She began to hum and then to sing in the silver tongue and her song brought to mind the green boughs of great trees rustling in the wind and the heady smell of flowers swaying in the breeze. She sung a sad song and although the words weren't understood by anyone there, the melody was well-known to all; it was *Love Avenged*, the epic poem that told the tragic tale of the demigod, Androktetes. It told of his failure to slay Orrymanthea, a dragoness and his greatest foe, when first they clashed. She had laid waste to an entire kingdom and she was also responsible for the abduction of Androktetes' love, Xanthippe. The poem culminated with the final battle between Demigod and Dragon and it ended with Androktetes victorious but heartbroken and alone, mourning his lost love. The sylfaea sung Androktetes' soliloquy and some of the chalyvoi sung the words they knew in their own tongue. The song ended with the Son of Hecate's pain and loss poured into the forging of the sword that he named Sorrow and all had to dry tears from their cheeks and their eyes. The chalyvoi murmured their appreciation of her singing.

Alopex had never heard this part of the poem before and he didn't understand the words but the melodious sadness conveyed by Silido-ra's voice had made his heart weep but his eyes had stayed dry. He was happy to see that Malus was moved by the song. The man of silver could not shed tears but emotion showed clearly on his face and pos-ture. After the song ended, the chalyvoi put out their pipes, emptied them, cleaned them and rose to pick spots to lay their bedrolls and go to sleep. Only Chryssa and the talls remained seated around the fire. The chalyvaea fed more wood to the fire and continued to smoke her pipe. Nargi picked a spot near the fire and laid down to watch this impromptu council between the eldest and the questors. Chryssa and Alopex studied each other and it was the danaos who spoke first.

"It is time to speak of the foe that plagues your polis. What is the tale behind this monster?"

"The seeress told you nothing then?" The chalyvaea asked in a voice both weary and curious. Her wizened face creased in a frown and even more lines criss-crossed her forehead.

"She told us that you face a terrible foe and she bid us to bring her one of the creature's eyes. Only then will she grant us an oracle." Silidora answered.

The sylfaea's voice was neutral but Chryssa caught the undercurrent of impatience and irritation. The eldest considered the weight of the truth and whether she should hold something back. In the end she opted for the simple and direct approach.

"Our foe is a *Panoptis*, one of the unholy spawn of the Mother of Madness and Argos of the Hundred Eyes. It is one of the most terrible of them all. It has and it is the *Eye of Death*."

Chryssa was pleased to see that her pronouncement brought a reaction from the three talls. Now that their foe had been revealed, their quest became at last a thing of weight and substance. Chryssa thought of their question as a cup that had thus far been empty but was now filling. But filling with what? Fearful aversion or heroic determination?

She continued, "The monster's tunneling encroached upon our own tunnels, a little more than a year ago when it breached an abandoned mine at the outskirts of the Hold, which had been converted into a mushroom farm. Since then, it has reached farther inside the polis."

"How do you fight it? Is it so terrible that an entire polis lies helpless before it?" Alopex asked and for the first time, Chryssa thought that he was paying attention.

"We do not fight it, not any more. We fought in the beginning. We sent warriors, accompanied by the few men and women versed in the Orphic Secrets, to find and slay the monster. When they failed, we sent more. We also hired freeblades, mostly danaoi from the Midlands. Our mountain kin also came from Ironcleft, when they learned of our troubles. Some of those who would go to slay the Panoptis would lose heart soon enough and return. Those were much less than the chalyvoi and the danaoi who honoured their word. However, it is from the cowards that we know how it is inside the tunnels created by the Panoptis because none of the brave returned. Unfortunately, none of the cowards went far except for one. That warrior went deep and fought the monster before he threw down his shield and fled. When he returned, he had gone mad."

"How many?" Silidora asked. The sylfaea's face had darkened and her eyes had an intensity that wasn't there before.

"More than three hundred have entered the tunnels of death and did not return. More than two hundred have died in the Hold during the darkcild's forays into our polis." Chryssa answered quickly, in a voice devoid of emotion and looked away. The hand holding the pipe trembled.

Alopex, Silidora and Malus were stunned by the chalyvaea's answer. They shared a look and waited for Chryssa to continue at her own time.

"Half the families in the Hold have been left with only one parent. The lives of many of my people who were in their prime, have been cut unjustly short." Chryssa said at length.

Alopex looked around him then and met the eyes of all chalyvoi with whom he shared this journey. They lay on their bedrolls but no one was asleep and no one spoke. They were all either middle-aged or old except for young Nargi who seemed embarrassed of that fact. Now the age of their companions made sense.

"When was the last warband sent?" Malus asked.

"That would be two and a half moons ago. A hero came to us from Ironcleft, Lothi Bronzehand. He arrived with his companions and there was much rejoicing in the Hold. He was the bearer of the heirloom of the Bronzehand clan, the *Scalecleaver*, an axe that bore a keen edge and mystical power. That axe had been crafted in the secret deeps of Ironcleft centuries ago, alongside the *Deephammers*. All chalyvoi of the Hold put their last hopes on Lothi's heart and his axe. Many of our own followed him as well. Hojar Rockspinner was one of those. He was the only one to return, half-mad from his ordeal in those tunnels of death. He told us the tale of a hero's death while he still had a tenuous grip on sanity. Lothi's death marked the end of our attempts to slay the Panoptis. Our last hope died with him."

"What have you been doing since? Surely you haven't given up? To surrender your polis to the foe, to endure his ravages is unconscionable. Do you see your polis as a monster's hunting ground or as a forge of heroes?" Alopex asked and his voice held the salty taste of judgment.

Chryssa would tell me later that this question, more than anything else, showed her who Alopex was and she was both sad and glad for what she'd seen in the danaos king. She was sad because he was young enough to weigh the plight of a people against their actions and find their actions as the heavier of the two. She was glad because he followed the path that the heroes of old had carved for themselves and for all those who would follow them; live or die matters not, it is the immortality you gain through your feats that matters. Alopex was unknown to her but he was carved of the clay that was used to make heroes, mixed with unquestioning courage and arrogant faith in one's self. He was a mirror to others - one that reflected a man's worth and feats in comparison.

"We haven't been idle, King Alopex. We bring down every passage where the tunnels of madness connect with ours. We build traps beyond the collapsed areas such as deadfalls and pits filled with pitch and we install a liquid fire projector that's always manned. We also line the passages with pitch and block them with tunnel-shields - wheeled platforms that carry a structure like a shield that blocks the whole passage - perforated so that warriors who shelter behind them can launch crossbow bolts and spears against the enemy. Some tunnel-shields carry light war machines such as scorpions. We have turned the monster back on many occasions, at great loss of life. What it comes down to however, is that the Panoptis cares not to invade the polis. If it wanted Glistenwall Hold, it would already have it. There are those who believe differently but I'm not blinded by either pride or hope. What the creature has been doing is raid the polis to kill and carry off some of the corpses..." Chryssa's voice broke in the end and she stopped.

Some of the chalyvoi turned their backs and faced the wall and some whispered invocations to the King of the Underworld for their loved ones. Alopex's face tightened and reddened from anger. What Chryssa described was anathema to all dorians. Men had been killed and if they bore no coin for the ferryman and their bodies hadn't been tended and buried properly by their kin, they were cursed to wander the shores of the river Acheron forever as lost souls.

"Do you know what the creature does with the corpses?" Silidora asked, although there could be but one answer.

I think that she hoped that the answer would be different - who wouldn't? Or perhaps, having walked with the demigod and having performed feats that had made her known across Dara Kadia, and perhaps beyond, she could guess at things that we couldn't imagine.

"No, we don't. No corpses have been recovered from the tunnels of madness and death. The cowards have never seen corpses or remains. Regardless, the answer is obvious. *The monster eats our dead.*"

Chryssa's voice carried her disgust for the Panoptis and still it wasn't enough, so she spat into the fire.

"We have built many pyres this last year because we do not have bodies to bury under stone. We make empty pyres and burn clay effigies, dressed in the clothes of the dead. The pyres are many and there have been periods when the fires were burning for days. The ash would rise high and fall down like rain. The families of the dead - most families of the Hold - smear their faces with ash these days."

Chryssa paused to smoke her pipe and her hands were shaking. She was held in the grip of a deep sorrow and she needed some time to compose herself before continuing.

"The danaoi that live on the skin and share the land with us, believe that we were greedy and careless and our tunneling in the earthdeeps awakened the monster. Many refuse to come to our polis or to associate with us any more, lest they attract the monster's attention. The people say of us that we carry the smell of the grave and they do not call my polis by its proper name anymore. They call it the *Hold of Ashes*."

Alopex saw some of the other chalyvoi brush a tear and Byrrna, who lay with her back turned to them, was crying.

"You have my sympathy for your troubles, Chryssa Goldheart. It seems that there is no end to the depravity of the spawn of the Dark Host. I have claimed the life of a Panoptis in the past but I haven't seen the like of what you describe." Silidora said.

"I have heard the tale. You were not alone in that deed."

Chryssa's comment hung heavy in the grim sorrow evoked by the words already spoken during that night council. It brought to the fore all the doubts of the chalyvoi. Alopex and Malus were unknown men and the Maiden of Mereandil was alone. Her feats, narrated and sung by minstrels all over Dara Kadia (and some of the songs were her own,) had been performed in the company of the Son of Hecate. But this time, he wasn't there with her. The elder locked gazes with the sylfaea and her eyes were full of doubt. She needed to hear that the dorians who had been given the quest, were the heroes who would see it through.

Alopex could feel the eyes of all the chalyvoi upon the three of them. Even Byrrna had turned to look at them, her eyes red-rimmed and puffy. He looked at Silidora; the sylfaea was hesitant because she was indeed alone and Chryssa had the right of it. The brother-king knew that the moment should not be left to wither in silence.

"Chryssa Goldheart, elder of Glistenwall Hold, I understand your doubts and fears. We can do nothing to alleviate them, other than give you our oath that we will not turn back from this quest. We will see it through to the end!" Alopex declared.

Silidora and Malus placed palm over mouth and gestured outward with palm open to show their acceptance of this oath as if they had spoken it themselves.

"Zeus, the Oathbinder hears your oath and so do I and will hold you to it." Chryssa responded in the proper form and thus sealed the oath bond that the questors and the chalyvoi of Glistenwall Hold now shared.

"Thank you, your oath is all we can ask for." Chryssa said and rose on creaking knees, signaling the end of this council.

The elder's bedroll was already made for her and she retired. She met the Nargi's eyes and the youth's gaze held a question. She shook her head slightly, signifying her denial and she laid down. Silidora retired as well. Alopex and Malus went outside together, to talk under the clear sky. Gray-bearded Drothas, whose braided hair were bound in copper wire, was muttering to himself as he stood guard at the entrance with spear in hand, wrapped in his heavy himation, trimmed with white fur. Respectful of their privacy and eager for some warmth, he withdrew inside the cave to sit and smoke by the fire and left them to talk and watch while they were outside.

Drothas had heard what had been said in the council. He had his doubts about all of them. Were they heroes? Were they the ones that would come back from the tunnels where all others had perished? Only the Moirae could answer that. Their resolve to perform this quest and their oath marked them as dorians of courage and worth but that wasn't enough. Drothas had seen many dorians of courage and worth leave for the tunnels. None had survived the gaze of the Eye of Death.

"I wish that we'd go faster."

Alopex's comment grated on the nerves of Eveder Goldnugget. It was only the tenth time that day that he'd heard the tall speak his fondest wish for this journey. He spat on the ground and said without turning to look at him, "We walk down a mountain covered in snow. The journey will take eight days with both legs unbroken and twenty with one leg broken. I prefer the quickest of these options."

Eveder didn't think much of the three talls. Alopex and this strange, silver fellow who was absent most days, he knew not at all and neither did any other. He had heard of the kingdom of Chalkaea years ago but only because it had a chalyvos for a king, a Wheelcopper from Dorgobek. He hadn't heard of this business of two brother kings succeeding the chalyvos king. The Maiden of Mereandil was known to all, but in all the stories she was Androktetes' companion. Now, she was alone and wasn't at all happy with the quest. She was sullen and as impatient as Alopex. Apart from the song in that first night, she had neither sung again, nor played a note on flute or lyre during the nights. In all the tales, the Maiden was joy and laughter to her friends and death to her foes. Now she was only sorrow and impatience. Eveder couldn't see how these three could defeat the monster that was devouring his city alive. Better men and women than them had tried and failed.

The Seeress of Glass spoke for the Mother of the Olympians but she had ignored the plight of Glistenwall Hold. In all their time in the temple, she'd given no oracle to them and in the end she'd sent these three, so-called heroes, on this quest instead. In Eveder's mind, the non-existent oracle's meaning was clear; the Gods had abandoned them.

As it was, someone did break his leg. It happened early in the fourth day of the journey when Eveder went to wash and fill his waterskin at the Zarotas river that they'd been following since that morning. It was a stony shore, ringed with boulders that the river had carried down the slope. The boulders that formed the banks and the rounded pebbles that made up the bottom of the river were slick with moss. The old chalyvos was careless, he slipped, his left foot lodged at an angle in a hollow between two stones and as he fell forward, his left leg from the knee down stayed where it was and couldn't rotate. Eveder didn't scream from pain when he felt tendons and muscles being torn but he shouted plenty afterward, a rich litany of curses, profanities and complaints about today's youth (Eveder always complained about the young generation). Tyche was often mentioned as well - not in kind terms - surely drawing the irate eye of the Goddess of Luck, as if his bad luck wasn't enough already.

"Look what you've done, you old fool." Chryssa wasn't in the mood for mothering her not-much-younger cousin. "We must splint the whole leg and you shouldn't put weight on it. I'm afraid we'll have to carry you in a litter."

All the chalyvoi had gathered around Chryssa and Eveder. Alopex was away because it was his turn that day to scout ahead of the company, a duty he shared with Silidora. It helped them use their nervous energy and seek the solitude that they both seemed to prefer. Malus was absent, as usual. The strange man of silver would always be gone in the morning and he would appear in the afternoon, when the company halted to make camp.

Silidora heard Chryssa and her face darkened. She was in a somber mood ever since she'd embarked on this quest. She felt that she was running out of time. She hadn't made the long journey to the Temple of Glass so as to fight in this quest but to receive an oracle to guide her in saving Androktetes. This foolish accident was another delay. She left the chalyvoi to fuss over the old man and went to be by herself.

She took out a wooden flute, beautifully carved with birds in flight. She closed her eyes and brought the flute to her lips. The melody began slowly as she reached into the Harmony, what most students of the teachings of Orpheas called the Aether. She drew power into her music, gave it a name and composed a minor spell, a secret she had discovered herself when she was but a child. Her simple melody wove with the Harmony and it sounded right. She opened her eyes and a woodpecker had perched on her flute. She stopped playing but the melody took a little longer to fade. She whispered a few words to her - it was a female bird - and sent her to find the fox-named man. The woodpecker found him about two kilometres ahead, going down a gentle slope, amidst the first snowbells of spring, purple-leafed flowers that had pushed through the thinning cover of snow. She perched on the man's shoulder and chirped the words she had been given. Then the magic left her free to resume her daily routine and she flew away.

When Alopex got back, he found the chalyvoi busy at building a litter. Eveder's left leg was bandaged and splinted and he was quiet despite the pain. Chryssa had filled his pipe with sunweed to deaden his pain and the old chalyvos was in that curious mood between sleep and euphoria.

"Wonderful. We just lost half a day." An exasperated Alopex said to Silidora in a low voice.

"We'll lose more days if we have to carry old Eveder. We can't afford such a delay." She looked him in the eyes, her meaning was clear. He had to do something.

Alopex knelt beside the injured man. Eveder looked at him with suspicion and consternation.

"Hey old-timer, I hear you had a bit of bad luck."

"Aye Brother-King, that I had. I'm afraid that I'm going to be a burden for the rest of the journey." A deep sigh followed, Eveder's regret was sincere. "I expect this to hurt worse than a night of bad ale, come tomorrow."

"It sure will." Alopex said as he examined the splint and the chalyvos' leg. He gingerly prodded the injured knee while asking Eveder how it had happened. Then he removed the splint, caught the lower leg under one arm and began moving the leg to test the knee-joint. Eveder bit his lip in pain but he endured the king's ministrations patiently. When he was done, Alopex carefully set Eveder's leg down and the chalyvos let out a long breath.

"Eveder, the injury is serious. You'll walk again but it will take a month at best before you can walk with a cane, a few months more before you can stand on your own and your leg will be weak and unsteady for the rest of your days."

"What do you know about such things? Chryssa is a wise woman and she didn't tell me that it was that bad." Eveder didn't appreciate today's youth talking like they knew everything, even if the one doing the talking was a king.

"I didn't want to cause you more grief Eveder but what Alopex said is true." Chryssa's tone was softer this time.

The old chalyvos began to curse his luck again. Silidora watched with interest the change in Alopex as he talked to Eveder and examined him. Despite his impatience and exasperation, his voice and manner was friendly and he was honestly concerned. Alopex stopped Eveder's tirade and name-calling with a gesture.

"I think Tyche has heard enough from you. This is actually your lucky day."

"Are you daft Alopex? How can this be my lucky day?" Eveder harrumphed for emphasis.

"Because you rested your old bones instead of marching and got stoned on sunweed as well. Tomorrow though, you'll make up for lost time."

"Hah! Good luck with my marching tomorrow." Eveder said with smug irritation.

Alopex smiled his mischievous smile, "I make it a point to always be in the favour of the Goddess of Luck. Stay quiet for this, old-timer."

He also spoke to those gathered round, "Don't interrupt me please."

Silidora translated his words for the chalyvoi who didn't speak the copper tongue - not because it was really needed but to emphasize the point - and stood two steps behind Alopex as an obstacle to any interference. Chryssa stood beside her, curious. The brother-king poured water on his hands from his waterskin and touched his face and Eveder's face. Chryssa gasped softly. She knew that all healing magic began with water, it was one of the few things well-known about the secrets of healing. Alopex opened Eveder's furs and the shirt he wore underneath and placed both palms on his body. The chalyvos looked at Chryssa and she nodded reassuringly. He was plainly worried but he didn't complain and he didn't interrupt Alopex.

The brother-king closed his eyes and began to chant in a voice that was used to chanting. That's what all others saw and heard but for Alopex himself, it was an entirely different experience. It was, in his own words, *a transcendence of the self and a cast of his daimon into the River of Faith.* Alopex was there, on the mountain but a part of him rose and stepped into another place, a place above this world, a place on the slopes of the tallest mountain of all.

Imagine what he saw; above him, palaces and temples of white marble would shine under the bright sun. All structures were surely surrounded by groves of olive and fig trees and grapevines in rows. Meandering paths would weave between the buildings and the groves. He was at the shore of a mighty river of crystal clear water. He couldn't see the far shore and the flow of water was frothing over unseen rocks just below the surface. He knew that this river had its source at the peak of the mountain and that it passed each of the residences he could see high above, the Houses of the Gods. This was the River of Faith that flowed down the slopes of Olympus. He didn't hesitate to enter the water and he gasped because it was cold. He waded in up to his knees in the strong flow and he could feel the current pulling at him, trying to sweep him along. He didn't need to go any deeper for this healing. He cupped his hands, filled them with cold water and drank and so, he brought a little piece of the divine into the mortal world and he became a link in the chain between mortals and immortals.

The brother-king seemed to glow, even under the light of the noon sun. Eveder began to sweat and progressively he got warmer until he felt as if a flame had been kindled inside him. He cried out in pain and his right hand grasped Alopex's arm and squeezed. Silidora moved to pry his hand loose but the old man held on in a vice grip. The brother-king's brow was furrowed but his concentration wasn't broken. His eyes focused on something that only he could see, his lips moved without sound. Eveder breathed hard and his body tensed but he remained still.

Alopex lifted his hands - it was done. Both the injured chalyvos and his therapon relaxed. Their movements were stiff and they breathed hard but all was well. Silidora stood beside Alopex with her hand on his shoulder and Chryssa knelt beside Eveder and took his hand. The gathered chalyvoi drew closer.

"You're all right. Rise and walk." Alopex said and he stood up.

Chryssa helped Eveder up but her aid wasn't needed. The rest stared in wonder as he put pressure on his broken leg and got up. He walked around, a bit stiff but without pain or other discomfort. The chalyvoi clapped him in the back and exchanged light-hearted banter. It wasn't often that they witnessed such a miracle.

In the eyes of the gathered chalyvoi, Alopex had grown, he seemed larger somehow.

"Old timer, you must eat a hearty meal because your body gave much to mend your knee. Eat well and sleep. Thank the Gods for your good fortune and make sure to mention my name in your invocations and libations."

"That I will, *Alopex Hieros*. You have my thanks and you hold my debt." Eveder said with newfound respect for the young danaos.

A *Hieros*, a healer who could drink the water of the River of Faith was respected in every land where dorians walked, fought or made their homes.

Chryssa bowed to Alopex and said with sincere gratitude, "You are a holy man, high in favour with the Olympians. I thank you for what you did for my kinsman, Brother-King of Chalkaea."

"I was happy to help. I only regret the time we lost. In any case, it will be dark soon and it would be foolish to continue. Let's find a likely camping spot to pass the night and get the cook-fires burning, I'm hungry after healing such an injury."

The chalyvoi were quick to comply. A good spot to make camp was found, within a copse of evergreens where the ground was only lightly covered with snow. The company was quick to set up tents and to prepare as good a meal as their provisions allowed. They sat down to eat quite early and they had time to enjoy the night. When Malus arrived to the camp, he found laughter and merriment and a warm welcome where he had gotten suspicious glances the previous nights. That night, around the fire, the people of Glistenwall Hold, who were slow to trust and accept outsiders, counted among them not an unlikely trio of strangers but three friends. They even dared to hope that they counted among them the heroes who would put an end to the Eye of Death.

Chapter 2. The Hold of Ashes

Year 129 DT, month of the Eagle.
Mother's House.

He lay naked on the cold, hard floor of the pitch-black chamber. The eye on the back of his head opened first. It was bloodshot, the iris a deep purple. Then the large eye on his chest half-raised its eyelid, it was black and it wept blood. The eyes on his palms opened next, both were an angry red and looked about. All the rest of the eyes awoke, one by one. The eye on his chest, the largest one of them all, closed again and so did the eye on his back which was only a little smaller. One of the bulging eyes on his belly blinked to clear the blood that had trickled down. I speak of it as a man but it was not a man. Its hairless body was that of a tall, bulky man but it didn't have any genitalia. Its head was too big and its left arm smaller than the right. Its head, body, legs and arms were filled with eyes of many sizes and colours. Its skin was pale white and it glistened from the disgusting tears and the other vile liquids wept by the eyes.

It was a *thing*, a spawn of darkness that had inherited the semblance of a man's form by its progenitor, Argos of the Hundred Eyes, also called Panoptis. *He-Who-Sees-All* was the meaning of the word in the Celestial tongue. *Madness and Death* was the meaning of the word in the minds of its victims. Argos had been a Gigas, a primordial giant who was said to have a hundred eyes. He was murdered by Hermes at the behest of Zeus. When the Father of the Titans returned from his exile to reclaim Gaea and the Cosmos, he brought with him allies; the Dark Host we call them because one and all they crave the darkness and hate the light. One of them, perhaps the most loathsome of them all, beheld the light with her many eyes and she went mad. She saw the Earth and all living things and her mind broke at the sight because she was an alien creature of the cold, lightless void between the stars. She had never known warmth, nor love, nor joy and she was incapable of knowing such noble sentiments. She made it her cause to close all eyes in the Cosmos so that the light wouldn't be seen and therefore, it would cease to exist. She came to be known as the Mother of Madness.

That creature sought a consort to create a mortal race to do her will upon the world. She was drawn to the unhappy soul of the murdered gigas, Argos, because of his enmity toward Olympos and because of his many eyes. Argos hated the Olympians and any who served them, invoked their names or loved them. That alien creature and the murdered gigas both had a common enemy in Gods and mortals alike and that was enough for them to join in unholy union. The Mother of Madness took the Panoptis' dead seed and spawned terrible progeny of many eyes that imitated the blessed human form.

She weaned her darkcildra on madness and murder and taught them only to despise all those who have their eyes open to the light. Dorians call them Panoptes, many-eyed men that are not men, who have a thirst for the lives of all dorians and a depth of madness that's unfathomable by rational beings. But I have said enough. No more will I speak about these matters. To speak of things of the Dark Host for what they are, invites madness. Therefore, I will think and speak of the Panoptis as if he was a man and so should you.

Death-that-walks-in-tunnels-of-weak-stone rose, alert and awake. His many eyes could see in absolute darkness as well as a danaos could see in daylight and there was nothing around him, below him and above him that could escape the gaze of his myriad eyes. The only feature of this cavernous chamber was the house he had been building for his Mother. It rose high, almost touching the roof of the cavern and it sprawled haphazardly every which way. It was a misshapen, ugly and terrible thing built with bone and skin and eyes, all taken from his victims. It smelled of dried blood and rotten flesh. Flies swarmed over the grotesque house and buzzed everywhere in its rooms and corridors. The materials he'd used to build it had been taken from the corpses of slain dorians and slaughtered animals, although anything taken from the latter was next to useless for his purpose. He just enjoyed to kill, to tear apart the frail bodies of anything that lived on this earth. The house needed some work still, but it was almost ready. Beyond this cavern, the tunnels of the labyrinth were already prepared for her arrival. He was pleased because his Mother was pleased. Her approval of his work showed in the languorous motion of the still-unformed essence in his belly, where she gestated. She spoke to him and her voice was a cold wave crashing down from the void between the stars, it drowned out everything else and demanded his attention.

"You have done well, my Unmaker. My House is almost ready. Know that they come, the half-blind maggots that crawl upon this earth. They shall be the last to offer you their blood to spill and their flesh and bones and eyes to complete my house. The Olympians take heed of where they walk and what they do. One of them belongs to Hermes, he's a lackey of the God who slew your father. Hate them my child, close their eyes, break their bones as their Gods watch, and finish my House. Then I will come to fill this labyrinth with more of my spawn, more terrible cildra, like you. My Unmaker, be the death of the dorians before you lay down your flesh and your life for me. My Consort, let me tell you of how this earth shall be like when all eyes close and all things of life are snuffed out. How comforting the darkness will be when their very sun becomes a dead, cold thing of the void. Let me tell you of when the Cosmos itself is unmade..."

So it was with the Unmaker, whom dorians call Panoptis, and his unholy mother. Lost in a rapturous rapport with the Dark Goddess that had spawned his race and who used him to touch this world, the Panoptis waited for the coming of the last victims.

I will say no more of what I saw and heard and I would be happy to forget everything that I know of the Mother of Madness and her darkcildra. I cannot forget but I can keep the worst of the knowledge for myself so that it will be lost with me. I know that Zeus, King of the Olympians, approves of this and I call upon him to continue to shield my soul from all the things that mortals are not meant to know.

* * *

The Midlands.

The hilly, lush lowlands spread like a verdant carpet south of the Earthembars. The giants had done nothing with this land except use it as a ground for hunting and for grazing their herds. Krimasand's claim had been ignored by the dorians that had been colonizing this land for the last century and a half. We settled the hills and the fields and the underearth and expanded the borders of Dara Kadia, which is the dorian name for all the lands we hold east of the vast mountain range of the Stonewalls and south of the no man's land that is the Hornfang Forest. Although it is settled, this land that has no name remains wild. We call it the Midlands.

The only signs of civilization are the walled hamlets and the farm plots and animal pens that surround them. The dorians that call this land home are herdsmen, fishermen, hunters, farriers and trappers. None of them dares go alone to hunt or fish or tend his herd; they go in groups of at least three men and they go armed. The chalyvoi of Glistenwall Hold are miners. The Hold is the only polis in this land, the only bastion of civilization that generations of danaoi and chalyvoi have ever known.

There are a few sylfaen as well, in the dense woods to the east and south but they're rarely seen. Although the fey that live and frolic in the streams, the glades and the woods would laugh to hear this, the land is slowly but steadily being tamed. Soon, it will have a proper name and all the dorians that have been nurtured by this land will begin to share an identity.

But I digress; it took the company six days to go down the mountain and reach the lowlands. They remained within arrow-distance of the east bank of the great Zarotas river after they reached the foothills. The river turned to a south-easterly direction and the company went with it.

"Of course, the chalyvoi were here first. My grandmother, Gareanne Bloodwine, daul of Gadra, daul of Agranne Goldstone, was among the first to behold the Zarotas flow at the bottom of the chasm. That was a hundred and forty-six years ago." Nargi said proudly.

The young chalyvos was in good spirits so close to home and eager to talk to the talls about his lineage and his polis.

"The colonists from Ironcleft numbered about three hundred men and women, mainly of the Goldstone, Breadhands and Goldheart clans. They carved the living rock of the chasm and their work was good. Thus was born Glistenwall Hold and it has prospered - until recent times that is." Nargi's exuberance was smothered and he looked down.

"Rumours of your polis' beauty has reached even Mereandil Forest, on the other side of the Stonewalls. I am eager to see what you have built, Nargi Alewood." Silidora told him and smiled to the young chalyvos.

Nargi's spirits perked up again. It was no secret to anyone (although

Nargi would be shocked to hear it) that he'd been enchanted with the Maiden.

"I wouldn't have expected news of our fair polis to have traveled so far but it is good and well that it did." Chryssa said as she came up to join them at the head of the column.

Walking was easy now and they made good time. Malus was gone, as he always was during the day but neither Alopex nor Silidora had ranged ahead that morning. The sporadic sight of hamlets and farms had put them at ease. If there was danger along their path, there would be some warning of it.

"I hear that Nargi has been educating you about our polis and our people." The elder chalyvaea remarked.

"He hasn't said anything about the giants of Krimasand. Why did they allow dorians to settle on their land and the colonists from Iron-cleft to build a city even?" Alopex asked the elder but it was Nargi who answered.

"All dorians live under Solon's law and the giants as well, by Zeus' decree. The law states that a kingdom's claim reaches as far as the roads it has built. No dorian needs to ask the permission of the king of Krimasand since his claim on this land is unlawful."

"Be that as it may, the king could have ousted you from this land whether you recognized Krimasand's claim or not." Alopex said with a smile of amusement but Chryssa gestured in denial.

"He could try. The colonists from Ironcleft were the first here and we took a dare. I remember when I first laid eyes on the Axecleft and heard the roar of the great waterfall. It was a good place and I wanted to live there and search for Gaea's bounty under the skin. We had come in strength with soldiers and builders as many again as the colonists. The builders helped us make a start and the soldiers shielded us during those first years. By the time the giants knew of our colony, the city was already half-built and fortified. The truth is though, that the giants care little for this land. There is an old feud between Krimasand and the freeholds of the Earthembars and so they remain apart from each other and have little contact. Krimasand cared little about the Midlands - not enough to come in conflict with us. Glistenwall Hold prospered and more dorians, mostly danaoi as could be expected, arrived and settled on the skin."

"We know a sweet deal when we see one. The chalyvoi mine the deeps and we settle on the land, or the skin if you prefer, under the sun. It has worked for us dorians since time immemorial." Alopex said.

Nargi added that there were sylfaen in this land as well.

"I'd like to see the forests and talk with my kinsmen. When I am done with my heart's quest, I think that I'll walk this land of yours." Silidora stated.

No chalyvos sought to intrude by asking what her heart's quest was. Such a woman as she, never lay still and was ever on the paths walked by heroes. They would learn of it, when she had performed the feat and made a poem of it.

"The Gods will it that you get your wish, while this land is still trod by dorian feet, Silidora Windwhisper." Chryssa said.

The roar of the waterfall drowned every other noise. The Zarotas fell more than a hundred meters to the floor of the chasm that opened like a jagged wound on Gaea's body. Legend has it that during the Titanomachy, the God of War had fought the Titan Opladamos, who was master of all weapons, in this location. Storm-eyed Ares fought with a great axe and Opladamos with a kopis in one hand and a three-headed flail in the other. In the course of the battle, the Bane-bringer knocked the Titan down and he fell where the chasm was. Ares lifted his axe high with both hands and brought it down with all his might. He severed Opladamos' head and the force of the blow made the axe bite deep into the earth. When the God of War lifted his bloody axe, the earth was cleft and has remained so to this day. So this chasm came to be and this is why the chalyvoi who came here to found a colony named it Axecleft. The chalyvoi never got tired of telling and re-telling that story and the talls had heard it, with various degrees of detail and embellishment, at least once from each chalyvos, during the journey.

When he saw the chasm for himself, Alopex believed in the truth of the legend. The chasm's lips were jagged and its sides were quite smooth and angled inwards the deeper they went. The Brother-King had seen many wounds in his life, not few of those on himself, and this was exactly like the wound that a half-moon axeblade, notched from battle, would leave on a man. He turned the waters of the Zarotas red in his imagination and the vista before him became a bleeding axewound on Gaea's flesh. He probed with his mystical senses and tried to feel the land, tried to hear the cadences of the years that had gone by and sort between the myriad impressions. He was lost in things that he wouldn't remember afterwards, lost in impressions too fine and too remote to take them and make them memories. However, just as he was about to give up, just for one moment, he heard clearly a deep, furious

– 25 –

scream and a hideous sound as the earth shook and parted and he smelled blood. Alopex opened his eyes and smiled. There was power in the chasm, power of war and bloodshed. It slumbered in legend but it was there, all around him, distant but tangible. Had this power drawn the Panoptis to the Hold, he wondered. For that spawn of darkness to even tread this ground was blasphemy. Alopex wondered whether he could awake this power and use it against the monster.

"I guess that I'll find out soon enough." He said in a low voice to himself.

"What is it that you wish to find?" Malus asked him from behind and Alopex jumped.

He turned to look at his friend and he saw Eveder just a little way off, staring wide-eyed, his mumblings drowned by the noise of the waterfall. He guessed what the old chalyvos had seen.

"You enjoy this, don't you Malus?" Alopex asked and his friend smiled.

"One finds his amusement where he can. What were you musing about?"

"Damn but your ears could hear a pine needle falling on soft grass. The legend of the Axecleft is true my friend and the echo of divine deeds done in war and sealed in blood and death, can still be heard. Perhaps there is power here that can be turned against our foe. We shall see."

Eveder could hear nothing of the exchange between the two talls but he kept a wary eye on the man of silver. He hadn't seen him coming but suddenly he was there! Eveder had his suspicions about Malus. The journey back had been too easy. The mated manticores that had harassed them on their way to the temple, never even made their presence known on the journey back. On the third day out, they'd found goblin tracks and smelly, goblin warrens but no goblins. They were a large and well-armed party but even that was no surety of safety. He was too old to be curious, however. All of them had reached the Hold in one piece and that was the important thing. The secret of the man of silver was his to keep or give away and he'd done no wrong. 'Live and let live,' as his father used to say.

Eveder went to the lip of the chasm and took an item out of a pouch - a finger-sized chunk of pink quartz. He threw the stone in the Axecleft, much as all other chalyvoi had done. They offered gifts to the River-God to thank him for the safe return of their company. He held no grudge for his leg either. After the offerings were given, the company made for the entrance to the Hold. A small fort rose midpoint along the Axecleft's length on the northern lip of the chasm alongside which they walked. The guards admitted them inside and there were long-winded greetings and many questions. After some time they were taken to a roofed, paved terrace with a crenelated stone railing at the edge of the yawning chasm.

The river could be heard singing the song of water at the bottom. A curious, cylindrical column of bronze, half an arm's length thick with symmetrical grooves, rose a few steps away from the end of the terrace's left side. A wooden platform with railing all around except the side facing the terrace, which it adjoined, seemed to be supported from this column. There was a railing on that side as well but it lay on the floor. Across the chasm, on the other side of it, a similar fort could be seen, guarding a similar stone terrace and another bronze column and wooden platform. On each side, the ten-meter high column reached all the way down to another terrace built on the face of the chasm. The far side of the chasm was dotted with windows, doors, ledges and balconies. The chalyvan city seemed to be built four or five levels deep, the topmost level connected to the fort via the curious columns. At the lowest level, chain bridges with wooden slats linked the two sides of the chasm and therefore, the two halves of the Hold.

Chryssa stepped onto the platform and the rest of the chalyvoi followed suit but the talls were reluctant to step onto this contraption.

"Unless you plan on flying down, you'd better do as we do." Chryssa advised the talls with a dry tone and a slight smile.

Malus stepped onto the platform first, Silidora followed him and looked at everything with genuine wonder while Alopex stepped onto the platform reluctantly and looked at everything with suspicion. Nargi and Drothas lifted and locked the railing on the open side of the platform and one of the guards pulled on a brass chain twice. A heavy bell was heard tolling somewhere below, twice, in time with the pulls on the chain. Before the tolling had ceased, the column began to spin and with a slight grinding sound, the platform lurched suddenly. Alopex and Silidora, who were looking down, grabbed the railing but after the initial jerky start, the platform performed a smooth descent.

"By the Gods, this isn't a column, its a giant screw!" Alopex exclaimed.

"Well, that's a good enough description of the helical column." Nargi said with amusement and some pride.

"The inventiveness of the chalyvoi is a wonder to behold. I had heard of such devices, but never seen one." Silidora remarked in the golden tongue and all chalyvoi seemed to gain a few fingers of height.

The descent was brief and the platform came to rest on a level with the balcony at the bottom of the helical column. A bronze, double gate led inside the city and presently it was wide open to the plaza beyond. A crowd of chalyvoi awaited their arrival. Two elders were at the forefront of the crowd and both wore their robes of office; brown with gold trim, marked on the chest with a blue rhombos and a black axe inside it. One of the elders was a woman of coppery-red skin that was like old leather while the other was a bald man with a long and scraggly beard, bushy eyebrows and too many lines on his face.

"Chaire travellers, we rejoice for your safe return." The elder held before him a gem-studded walking cane in a slightly-shaking hand as he welcomed them.

The newly-arrived chalyvoi, except for Chryssa, touched left palm on right breast. Chryssa walked forward and greeted first the man and then the woman in the chalyvan greeting of both arms clasped at the forearms.

"It does my heart good to see you, Paregos Goldarm son Dareg. It does my heart good to see you, Promexa Breadhands daul Nura."

"You were gone for so long, Chryssa. You left during Lyra's star-bright and it is now the turn of the Eagle. We thought that you were lost to us." Promexa said in a voice that conveyed her concern.

"The Seeress of Glass was particularly demanding. She kept us at the temple for three weeks before giving us the word of Godmother Rhea. The journey wasn't easy either but at least we faced no real danger."

"What of the oracle, Chryssa Goldheart daul Kendra?" Paregos asked with a tremulous voice and all mutterings and conversations died down. One and all, the chalyvoi quieted and awaited to hear Chryssa's answer.

"I ask for the council of elders to be convened and it is there that I shall speak of the oracle."

There were mutterings and unease in the crowd at Chryssa's reluctance to reveal the prophecy. The elders didn't press her further however.

"So be it then. Let's walk to the council hall together. I'm sure that the rest of the councilors are eager to hear you and will arrive immediately."

A few words from Paregos sent a dozen chalyvoi to carry word to the other councilors of the meeting. Chryssa motioned to the talls to accompany her and told her fellows, "I bring these dorians to the council hall. They are part of the future of our Hold. We journeyed together from the Temple of Glass."

"We thought that they were freeblades engaged by you for the journey." Promexa told Chryssa in a low voice.

"Not so." Chryssa said and addressed the crowd. "Citizens of our polis, we have distinguished guests."

The elder introduced the three talls with full titles and it caused quite a stir. The crowd parted for the three elders and the talls to proceed to the council hall. The rest of the newly-arrived chalyvoi joined their kin and greeted their families but they refused to speak of the non-existent oracle. Chryssa had asked them to keep it secret until she had discussed it in council.

The crowd followed the elders and the talls through the streets, tunnels and plazas of the polis. The walk gave Alopex, Silidora and Malus time to study the city and discover the origin of its name. Many surfaces throughout the city such as tunnel and building walls, floors and even ceilings, were adorned with glistening mosaics. Alopex noted with interest that the mosaics glistened under even the faintest light not just because of the glass and ceramic tesserae; there were gold tesserae and even small gems inlaid within them.

Silidora noted his interest and caught the gleam in his eye. She didn't worry overmuch because they were oathbound to perform this quest and they could not afford to fail. He wouldn't have the opportunity or the temerity to try to pry out some of the gold and the precious stones from the mosaics, under the circumstances. At least, she hoped so.

At this point, I should introduce myself. I am Rathi Breadhands and I was one of those who abandoned everything when I heard from a customer that Chryssa Goldheart had returned and that she'd brought guests of quality. I left my wife to mind the bakery and went to hear the oracle that the elder had surely brought back. I went to the Plaza of Ancestors and found it already crowded. I got my first look on the three talls from afar as they were led to the council hall. The Maiden of Mereandil was a sight I didn't expect to see in my lifetime. I always imagined her to be larger than life but she was only a petite sylfaea - a rare sight to be sure but too small to fit my imagination. The danaos king was pretty plain and unimpressive and the third tall - the captain of the king's royal guard - was cloaked and hooded, his arms hidden. People said that he wore a silver mask or even that he was a man of silver!

The account of the journey of Chryssa's company to the Temple of Glass and back was spreading from mouth-to-mouth and I heard a hodge-podge of rumours regarding the whole thing. The presence of the talls was also the subject of intense speculation. Everyone had his own explanation and loud arguments broke out in the plaza after the doors of the council hall closed. Many maintained that the hooded man was the Son of Hecate. I didn't believe the rumour since the Demigod had no reason to hide from us, since his companion was here. As for the other two, if that young, fox-named danaos was a king and the other one was made of silver, then I was Dagmeros Soulhammer, working adamantite in Hephaestos' own forge!

There was nothing to do but wait and I was in no mood to hear any more tall tales or spread them around. I went to the Smiling Beard tavern and I was in luck; there was a chair empty at a table which four others shared. I got the guarded look from two of them but I was used to such looks. I'd been getting them often enough in the last few months. I pretended not to notice. When one man from Chryssa's company came into the tavern, every man and woman from every table shouted and offered to buy him drink in return for him sitting at their table to speak of the journey. It quickly became a contest with the patrons offering more and more horns and kantharoi of beer, ale and cider until Nargi Alewood promised to tell the story to all and a chair was set on top of the barkeep's counter.

The lad sat there, somewhat uncomfortable from all the attention, to tell his tale. We all stayed quiet, except to ask questions when Nargi paused for a sip. He was quite taken with the talls, especially the beautiful sylfaea with the enchanting voice. The others were indeed a young king of a kingdom I'd only heard of some years ago, because its previous king had been a chalyvos. That kingdom surely suffered for the exchange, I thought then. Nargi went on to recount that Alopex, called Dawnblade, had been crowned by the great thane of Dorgobek and that he was also a holy man who carried favour with the Olympians! There were guffaws and laughter and Nargi went quite red with embarrassment and irritation. He was the youngest of Chryssa's company and his description of Alopex sounded outrageous. A dorian such as him should have been known throughout Dara Kadia yet he was unknown, as was his brother, Glaucos. The third dorian was an uncanny man of silver who had been barred from entering the Temple of Glass and who was often absent during the journey back. Some, who still entertained the idea that the hooded man was the Son of Hecate, were crestfallen when they heard that.

I toasted Dagmeros silently, spilled some beer on the floor and begged his forgiveness for my earlier presumption. Nargi was forbidden from revealing what the talls were doing in our polis but I'd learn that soon enough. I was so engrossed in Nargi's story that I nursed a single kantharos of axebite dark all the time that I sat there. The more I heard about the talls, the more I became certain of why they had come. One last foray into the cursed tunnels of the Panoptis, with them carrying the torch of our hopes for the Nightson's defeat. As my certainty grew, so did my determination to join them. I was tired of living without my heart and without my pride. I had left both in the Panoptis' cursed tunnels and I had to find them again.

No one had spoken ill of me, not my wife or my parents or any of my kin and neighbours. When I or any of the others like me, entered a shop or a tavern or took part in a conversation about the troubles of the Hold, we'd get the look and the conversation would turn to some other topic. Sometimes, we got together but the conversation never turned around to what we had in common. Everybody coped with his shame as best he could and tried to forget it. I couldn't forget. I was soaked in cold sweat from even thinking of returning to the tunnels and my stomach felt like it had fallen in a pit, but I had to do this. Better dead than a coward. The future would be grim for Lorna, Piria and little Lothi if the Panoptis wasn't destroyed. They'd be refugees soon and when that happened, I wouldn't be able to live with myself.

Cries from outside brought me out of my black thoughts. Hojar Rockspinner had been called to the council hall. I didn't rush out to watch like all the rest; there was nothing to see in that sad wreck of a man. But I didn't want to be the only one who had stayed in the tavern so, I too went out to watch after a while. Hojar's wife walked with the poor wretch, and guided him slowly, because of his bad leg and his stumbling steps. He would try to go another way every few steps and Ferna would gently keep him walking in the right direction. He stared in confusion at everyone around him. I felt pity for him, every step of the way until the council hall's doors closed behind him and I returned to my seat.

The council elders would address Hojar with respect but he wouldn't respond. Sometimes he would cry or drool. The talls would be surprised to hear that the white-haired old man they saw before them, was a man in his prime, as far as years counted. A man who until recently was considered the best minstrel in the Hold. Now he couldn't eat or piss without aid. Ferna would actually be the one to recount her husband's story. The story of the only dorian that fought the Panoptis and lived to tell of it. The tale of the last punitive expedition against the thrice-cursed monster. The death of our last hope. I knew the tale that Ferna Rockspinner daul Madvi would recount before the council and the talls. Every citizen of the Hold had heard it and repeated it a hundred times.

It was five months ago when the great warrior, Lothi Bronzehand, arrived to Glistenwall Hold from our mother-polis, the proud Ironcleft, with his companions. He came to slay the Panoptis and there was much rejoicing in the Hold. Lothi was the bearer of the heirloom of the Bronzehand clan, the *Scalecleaver*, the mystical axe crafted in the secret deeps of Ironcleft when the dragons still ruled the world. Eight citizens of the Hold were added to Lothi's companions and Hojar was one of them. He was brave and he wanted to be the one to craft the epic tale of the Nightson's destruction. We don't know the details of what happened during the exploration of the tunnels. When Hojar returned to us he was half-mad already and he got more incoherent by the day until his mind was gone completely. Ferna would tell them that Hojar had spoken of a madness that affected them all, some more than others, the longer they were in the tunnels and the deeper they went. He had spoken of paintings of madness and of things of bone that claimed the lives of some of the companions and the sanity of the rest. No one knew anything about the things he'd spoken about.

When Lothi's company finally met the Panoptis and did battle with it, all of them met their deaths. Hojar was the only one who survived, because he fled in terror. Overcome by a mad fear, he had ran away. However, at some point he'd mastered himself and cursing himself for a coward, he'd ran back to the battle. He saw Lothi from afar, fighting the monster alone, the corpses of his companions strewn around, one of them still alive but with his left arm torn out, laughing madly as he bled to death. The Panoptis bled a foul green, glowing blood from many wounds and many of its eyes were destroyed by blade, hammer and bolt. One spear was impaled in its back. It was a mark of how close Lothi and his company had come to defeating the foul darkspawn. *Scalecleaver* had endured the unmaking of the Panoptis' gaze and with it, the hero had struck mighty blows upon the monster. Lothi's body was criss-crossed with open, bleeding wounds from the power of the Panoptis'eyes to unmake flesh as well as wood and metal and stone.

The hero stood proud and strong, despite his wounds and despite the fact that he was the last. He fought to the end.

Hojar, wounded and terrified, tried to reach Lothi's side. He never did manage it. He saw the Panoptis' largest eye, the one on his chest, opening and he felt as if nails were driven into his eyes and a piercing pain wracked his whole body. He was two stone-throws away and that was what saved him. He halted, closed his eyes and covered his face with his hands and then heard Lothi's anguished scream. His death scream. Stricken with grief and despair, Hojar fled again. He never looked back to see Lothi's corpse. Somehow, he made it back alive. His account lacked much; he only said that he managed to reach one of the exits to the land's skin and then ran to the Hold, without stopping. He came to us on the sixth day after Lothi's company left the Hold. He came to us prematurely aged, his hair and beard white, his skin sagging and old, his eyes haunted, his mind broken. We all cried then and we despaired and kept the fires burning for a week, watching the ashes of our hopes rain down. A *Hold of Ashes* in truth.

I finished my beer in one gulp, left four chalkoi on the table and left the tavern and the plaza. I wasn't there to see the councilors and the talls after the council or hear them speak of the quest given to them by the Seeress of Glass. I had preparations to make.

Chryssa Goldheart had offered to host the questors for the night. When I got there, people were gathered outside her house, armed for battle. Their armours, shields and traveling packs had been surely left at the southern gatefort. These were the last soldiers of the Hold, the last of the brave. They eyed me with disbelief at first and then they ignored me. I saw the danaos they called the Fox, standing at a window on the second floor, looking out. They were gathered up there, making plans for the expedition and the battle with the foe and they were choosing the warriors that would accompany them. I had to lie about being on council business in order to be admitted inside the house. The elder's son, Kerin, took me to the living room where the questors conferred, left me at the top of the stairs and announced my arrival. I heard Chryssa tell Kerin to take my message and send me away. I went in.

"Forgive my intrusion, elder but I won't be sent away." I said.

I saw the three questors up close for the first time. All eyes were on me. The eyes of the talls were measuring me, judging me. They were the eyes of heroes who would walk into the tunnels of madness willingly and I was only a coward. Chryssa's eyes held contempt. I met her gaze and I was relieved because someone looked at me with sincere emotion - at last. I am a coward, look at me and see me for what I am! Strange as it sounds, Chryssa's contempt strengthened my resolve. I bowed to the assembled dorians.

"Chaire, Chryssa Goldheart daul Kendra and chaire, questors. I have come to declare my wish to accompany you in this expedition."

My voice betrayed nothing of my fear. I was proud of that, at least.

"There has been no call for companions in this expedition and there will be none. Go back to your wife and your children, Rathi." Chryssa said, rejecting my claim out of hand.

"My kin have died in those tunnels and the heirloom of the Bronze-hand clan, family of my family, is in the hands of a darkspawn. My polis is dying. I have every right and the moral obligation to accompany these questors."

Chryssa had a retort ready but before she could speak, Alopex got up and came to stand before me. There was something in the man just then, a hint of danger that made me want to step back but I held my ground.

"Are you so eager to die, chalyvos? Although the accepted tactic is to overwhelm a Panoptis with numbers, in this case we have decided otherwise. We won't lead the citizens of the Hold to a slaughter and we do not have the strength to spare in order to protect you from the doom that awaits in the monster's tunnels. Therefore, I think it best to put any notions about accompanying us out of your head. You have my promise that when we return, we'll bring this heirloom with us, if we find it. Otherwise, you'll search for it after the Panoptis has been slain and the tunnels are safe."

I couldn't believe what I was hearing. How did they expect to defeat a Panoptis, who was an Eye of Death no less, just the three of them? You had to bring as many warriors as the monster had eyes, to stand a chance against it. Dozens had to die for such a creature to be destroyed.

"There are twenty chalyvoi and ten danaoi out there waiting for the call, certain that you will lead them to the tunnels and you tell me that they wait in vain? Be that as it may, I am coming with you Brother-King of Chalkaea and I ask nothing but the chance to fight by your side. If you choose to reject me, I shall be there when you depart tomorrow and I shall chance to walk the same path as you."

That's what I told him and I crossed my arms to show my resolve. I registered a whip-quick movement barely before a bronze dagger was pressed at my throat. I hadn't even seen from which sheath it had been drawn from! I swallowed and kept my eyes on the king's face. He smiled condescendingly and sheathed his dagger.

"You're not much of a soldier, are you friend? I can smell the beer on your breath and you have flour all over your beard, hair and clothes. A baker's place is at his bakery, with his family. Leave this matter to us. It will all be better in the morning."

He turned his back to me. I burned with anger and I took one step forward and grabbed his arm. He turned, his surprise evident at being manhandled by a mere baker.

"I do not ask for your permission, Alopex Dawnblade, *I am telling you*. This is my polis and my life and it is my wish to risk it in the tunnels of madness!"

Alopex and I locked gazes for a while, until Silidora coughed. Alopex smiled then but this time it was a warm and mischievous smile.

"Well friend, you have the right of it. It is your life and your polis. You are welcome to accompany us." He added hastily, "I'm sure my companions won't have any objections," and looked at Silidora and Malus.

They both nodded their affirmation.

"That's it then. Be here at first light Rathi, armed and ready."

Just like that, I was accepted, dismissed and doomed to a gruesome death. My first thought was of the inconsistent and exasperating character of danaoi but then the reality of the situation sank in and a chill went up my spine. I had just earned my right to die in the Panoptis' tunnels. A weight as heavy as a mountain had been lifted from my shoulders and I felt light again. I hadn't felt like that for a long time - too long. I grinned like a fool, mumbled a farewell, made a clumsy bow and left the house in a hurry. I had to get outside and breathe. Some of those waiting outside asked me questions but I barely heard them. I told them that they had gathered in vain, I felt that they had to know how lucky they were.

I slept well that night, without fear in my heart. I would know a constant fear and a mad terror in the tunnels ere long but that night, the mountain had been lifted and my heart was light and that was all that mattered.

Chapter 3. The House of Madness

Year 129 DT, month of Argo, Hephaestos' Noumenia.
The Midlands, Glistenwall Hold.

The sun had just risen over the horizon when the questors and I emerged from the gates of the southern gatefort. Alopex was armoured in a simple, unadorned linothorax with thick, leather vambraces and bronze greaves. He had his numerous bronze knives and daggers sheathed all over his person and carried a spear. He had added a chalyvan, steel xiphos to his arsenal. He looked more like a common footman than a king, truth be told. Malus wore nothing but a woolen himation and a leather cloak. He had no weapons except for a spear that one of the fort's guards gave him. It was bad luck to go into battle without one.

Silidora was splendid in her glossy black, promethean steel armour, that covered her from head to toe. Her armour was the envy of many a smith since the secret of the metal was known only to a few masters of the craft. That steel was so heavy that no one would believe that a woman such as her, petite and light, would ever wear armour made of blackiron. She carried a recurved long bow in one hand and a broad-headed spear in the other. *Defender*, the legendary sword that the Son of Hecate had given her as a gift, was sheathed in her waist, in a scabbard of lacquered ebony, covered in linen fabric, its throat and tip fitted with bronze which was etched with leaf-patterns. At last, the image of the Maiden of Mereandil had come alive before me! Just then, when she stepped into the sunlight, planted her spear in the ground and tested her bow string, she was a figure out of an epic poem, a resplendent amazon.

I was girded in a muscled, bell cuirass of bronze with greaves, helm and round shield. I wore a jerkin over the armour, for the pockets it had. My trusty warhammer was thrust through a handle-sheath sewn on my wide, leather belt and I carried a steel-tipped spear and a crossbow as well. The bolts were secured in a belt quiver, covered and bound with cord. We all carried necessary equipment for the exploration of the Panoptis' tunnels as well as food and water for four days.

Chryssa and the other elders, as well as a crowd, had gathered to see us off. The citizens of the Hold crowded the battlements and the grassy field just beyond the gate and some had even spread blankets on the ground and had baskets with bread, cheese, milk and wine to break their fast. Lorna was there, holding Piria by the hand, baby Lothi carried on a sling on her back. She hugged me and tears ran down her cheeks. I didn't cry. I could lie that I did it in order to appear brave in front of my woman and my daughter. The truth is that I didn't cry because I was terrified. The elation of the past night had ended and my nightmare had began. If I began crying just then, as I held my wife, I would lose all courage and shame myself. I preferred dry eyes and few words. We had said our goodbyes earlier, in our home.

Those who had gone to the Temple of Glass and had returned with the questors - young Nargi, old Eveder, cranky Byrrna and the others - were there to shake the hands of the talls, pat them on the back and speak heartfelt wishes for luck and success. They didn't forget to shake hands with me and wish me well but I could see it in their eyes; what they really expected of me was at worst to see me again before nightfall and at best an empty pyre. We were given kylixes and Chryssa poured wine for us. The questors and I poured half of the wine on the ground, as an offering to Hephaestos on this day dedicated to him and we drank the rest. After this sponde, we set on the road leading south.

I was glad to leave the scrutiny of my people behind me and get on the road. It was a narrow road, rutted from the small carts used by the people to carry their produce from the fields to the Hold and trade their goods. The sun shone on the land, the larks were singing and the air was alive with insects. The land was waking up from the winter and the spring flowers had just began to scent the world. The sky was a clear, stark blue and the clouds were a pure, unsullied white. I experienced everything vividly, like a man who sees it all for the first time – or the last.

"You know Breadhands, it's not too late to turn back." Alopex's voice was condescending and his words hit me both with the doom that awaited me ahead and the shame that I was leaving behind.

I looked at the young and arrogant danaos, not unkindly and without anger. When he accepted me yestereve, the mountain had lifted and I would not soon forget that.

"When you set your feet on the road, it's too late to turn them back, Brother-King. A poet said that and I take it to heart this day. I have no regrets, fear not. I will draw the Panoptis' gaze and so give you a chance to strike it a mortal blow."

I was surprised to find in myself the conviction that went into my words. I walked to my doom with a heavy step and fear had settled comfortably in the pit of my belly, but I did walk.

"Very well; lead on then and make haste. The sooner we see this quest through, the sooner your polis will be free from its doom and the sooner we can return to the temple to receive the oracle we asked for."

Bravado was a time-honoured tradition of soldiers going into battle. Alopex would have me believe that he'd face certain death with eagerness, without hesitation and seemingly without fear. He succeeded.

I led the questors to the nearest entrance from the skin to the tunnels. There were three such entrances spread within half a day's walk from each other. The one nearest to the Hold was just one kilometre and a half away, just far enough for a man to have enough time to think about what he's doing. Enough time to be conquered by his fear or to make peace with his fate. I found the entrance easily but it had changed. The opening in the earth that led down, had become a hole. It was a large hole that could swallow a large cart and the oxen pulling it. The ground fell into an abrupt descent into darkness. Although the sun was up, the light did not reach as far inside that hole as it should. It was as if that hole didn't lead below the skin but somewhere else, where it was dark and cold, a place that didn't belong to the Earth. Once again, I found myself standing before that maw that led to horror and death, paralyzed by fear and it felt just like the first time. Only worse.

The others got busy; they checked their arms, lighted lanterns and slung them on a pole and shed some light inside the hole. They secured a rope and threw it down the hole. They spoke to me but I didn't hear them at first. A slap on my helm brought me to my senses and I started.

"We're going inside Breadhands, care to join us?"

Alopex offered me the rope and he didn't look afraid. The others didn't look afraid either...they looked eager. All eyes were on me. I didn't trust myself to speak. I took a step and then another and caught the proferred rope. I went to the lip and slipped – careless. I held onto the rope and hand over hand, I descended into the maw. The first time, I'd made it only halfway down. When I stepped on solid ground it seemed to me that I'd spent an eternity going down a pit of Tartaros. It wouldn't occur to me until much later that I'd been the first to enter the tunnels.

The darkness was oppressive and it felt as if we'd been swallowed by an otherworldly beast. Behind us there was light, streaming down the hole but it seemed far away. The light of a quartet of storm lanterns, hanging from a pole carried by Malus, shed enough light to illuminate the tunnel for a few strides ahead and behind us but it wasn't enough. This place swallowed the light.

"Will you shed light on the darkness or should I?" Alopex asked Silidora.

Instead of a response, the sylfaea whistled in perfect imitation of a sparrow and raised her right arm before her, with forefinger extended. A mote of light was kindled above her finger and grew and took the shape of a luminous sparrow that fluttered about briefly and came to rest on her finger. The sylfaea brought it close to her lips and whispered a few words to the mystical bird which immediately took flight and hovered about fifteen strides ahead of us. A good stretch of the tunnel was illuminated by the sparrow and no enemy would catch us unaware as long as the bird of light flew ahead of us.

"What do you think Malus?" Alopex asked.

"I hope it doesn't narrow down. Not big enough but I'll do what I have to." The man of silver answered and Alopex only nodded.

I had no idea what they were talking about but I didn't inquire into their affairs. We assumed formation and began a cautious exploration of the tunnel. Silidora and Alopex were positioned at the front and near the walls, across from each other while Malus and myself were five steps behind them, walking side-by-side at the center of the tunnel. Malus carried the pole from which the four lanterns hung while I held my loaded crossbow with both hands, ready to shoot.

The tunnel's walls, floor and ceiling were like nothing I'd seen before. They were full of uneven surfaces and jutting planes. The floor was strewn with debris and it was stepped or angled every two or three paces. It felt like walking on a crooked stairway that went neither up, nor down. The ceiling never reached lower than three metres and a half. So many nooks and crannies and jutting surfaces blocked or absorbed the light shed by the lanterns and that of the light sparrow, and created patches of shadow all along our line of vision. The tunnel had the expected musty smell of damp earth but it also had a feeling of weight, of a load pressing down upon me. I had heard of such feelings in sylfaen and danaoi, when they walked below the skin and I had often joked with other chalyvoi about such weakness. Now, it was my turn to feel what I once had ridiculed.

"This is the ugliest tunnel I've ever walked in." I said, keeping my voice low, almost whispering.

It was true that our light was a dead giveaway to any creature ahead of us and that there was no need for whispering but sound carries farther than light and round corners. Whispering while in the deeps, is a habit instilled in every chalyvos.

"This is a patchwork tunnel of mismatched and ill-fitted pieces. A madman's work." Alopex said in an equally low voice.

"A curved patchwork of mismatched pieces." Silidora added. "You and Malus cannot see it Alopex since your eyes cannot penetrate the darkness but the tunnel curves gently. It's so strangely built that I can't be sure though. Rathi do you see it?"

"I do. The tunnel ahead has an obvious curve to the right but I didn't really expect otherwise."

"How so?" Malus asked.

"I've heard accounts of these tunnels from Hojar and a few others and had time to think about them. The Panoptes are neither diggers nor builders. They're destroyers that unmake the stone and the earth around them as they unmake the weapons and the armours of their enemies; as they unmake the lives of the warriors who dare face them. I didn't expect such a creature to excavate tunnels in straight lines or with any sense of planning or design." I answered.

I was wrong but I couldn't have known that then. The tunnel ran for a good distance, always curving to the right which I came to consider the inwards direction. Our progress was slow as we moved cautiously and made frequent stops to listen for any signs of a presence ahead or behind us. No one could be behind us, since we had found no side-tunnels leading away from the one we followed but we were alert to such an eventuality regardless. There isn't such a thing as being too cautious when exploring a monster's lair.

I paid careful attention to the walls as we walked and was disappointed every time that I found a mark. All chalyvoi and surely most, if not all of the danaoi that had walked in this tunnel before us, had left chalk marks on the walls. It was standard practice for underground exploration. All the chalk marks that I found were incomplete half-disks that indicated the passing of dorians and the direction but not one was marked full by someone who returned. We didn't bother making our own marks. After all, we would be the last to walk those tunnels. After what we estimated to be a four-hour walk, we stopped to rest.

"The Panoptis surely aims to kill us with boredom." Alopex said as he ate an onion with a slice of hard cheese.

"What is the use in excavating a long corridor?" Malus wondered aloud. "There's no point in this tunnel and the time and energy it required to be made are staggering." He added.

The man of silver had propped the lantern-pole on the wall. Early in our exploration, he had doused three of the lanterns and had left only one lit to conserve oil.

"Perhaps the creature is mad." Alopex said and laughed at his jest.

"There's no doubt about that in the minds of all those who have faced such monsters and lived to tell the tale. Their madness is no laughing matter." Silidora said in the annoyed tone that she reserved for the young king.

"No one who fought the Nightson, ever returned." I said in a voice that was too loud.

They all looked at me with concern. I was more nervous than any of them and I'd been on edge ever since we entered. Twice during our progress down the long tunnel, I shot my bolts at stones and shadows, because I thought that something was there. Even when we rested, I was sitting with my loaded crossbow propped on my knees and held with one hand, pointed at the darkness beyond. I ate bread without appetite and I tried not to show how afraid I was but of course, it was evident to all.

"That much we already know, Rathi." Alopex said.

"Only Hojar returned and he wasn't of a mind to mark his passing if this was his route to the surface." I said.

Alopex was worried about me, I could tell. He thought that I would snap sooner or later. If I was in his place, I'd prefer that it happened sooner rather than later.

"You will be the first to do so, Rathi Breadhands. Upon our return, you shall fill all the half-moon marks." Silidora said, intending to comfort me, bless her heart.

Alopex didn't want to continue feeding my fears and so he changed the topic in his usual light-hearted manner.

"I'm bored of this. Perhaps we should begin yelling, attract its attention, fight it and be done with the whole thing."

All eyes turned to him and he shrugged, still chewing. "We'd be done with the darkspawn and be back to the Hold in time for dinner."

"I think it's best if you endure the boredom just a little while longer." Silidora remarked dryly.

"I'm not in a hurry to confront the Panoptis' eye of death, if you must know." Malus added.

"I imagine you wouldn't be, my friend, and I wish I had a better plan than this but it stands to reason that the darkcild will turn its gaze of death upon the greatest threat."

The questors had obviously made plans to which I was not privy and I did not consider myself an equal member of this company so I did not demand to be informed of them. What worried me was Silidora's look when she looked at Malus. There was pity and doubt in her eyes. It was she that rose first and signaled the end of our rest and of the discussion.

When we found the hole, we were as tired as after a day's walk on the skin. Alopex and Silidora couldn't tell whether eight hours or ten or twelve had passed but I knew that we'd spent about eight, perhaps nine hours just walking along that interminable tunnel. We'd found no branching corridors, no features at all since we'd entered that strange, impossibly long tunnel. What we did find was a huge hole, as big as the one that led into this tunnel from the skin. It didn't mark the end of the tunnel because on the other side of the hole, it continued on. The hole filled the whole floor and a man's height of soil and stone had been unmade in order to create it. Another tunnel opened under the hole, the floor of which was about five metres below. Chalk marks indicated that dorians had gone down this hole before us. None had come up and there was no rope or anything else to show us how they'd descended.

"This hole is such a relief that I could cry." Alopex said as he crouched at the lip of the hole and looked down.

He echoed the feelings of all of us.

"I thought we'd do nothing but walk this cursed corridor for the rest of our natural lives."

Silidora was tired and a headache had begun to throb behind her eyes some time ago, judging from the way she rubbed them regularly.

"I don't think that it's wise to continue past this point. We need rest. First we will check the lower tunnel and if there's no imminent danger, then we'll return up here to sleep in shifts."

"Sounds like a plan. Ladies first?"

The king's jest was lost on the sylfaea who gave him a tired look. She extended her finger for the light sparrow to perch and she blew softly on it, making it disperse into light motes that winked out. Darkness enveloped us and was kept at bay only by the single lantern.

"Your turn, Alopex." She said.

"In that case, I go first, then Malus."

Alopex cupped his hands together and invoked the Sun God to light his way. He repeated his invocation with conviction a second and a third time, until a light was born inside his cupped hands. It was a sun the size of a river pebble and the brother-king's smiling face was lit with a warm, white brilliance. He opened his hands and the tiny sun dropped down the hole and hung in the air, illuminating the tunnel below. It went in both directions and it ran at an angle to our tunnel. That was all we could see from above. Some debris seemed to litter the floor and the lip of the hole was broken and scraped at places by something heavy that had gone down. There were some dark splotches on the floor below that we all agreed could have been dried blood. Silidora also smelled a faint stench that she couldn't identify.

Malus drove two bronze pitons into the ground with a hammer whose head was wrapped in leather strips to minimize the noise. Then he tied a rope around them and threw the length of it down the hole. After that, he crouched at the lip of the hole, beside Alopex and waited. We stayed silent and quiet and listened. The only sound was that of a rivulet of water running down the wall somewhere below, making little splashing noises.

"Can you hear it?" Silidora whispered.

I couldn't hear anything at first but after a while, there were thumping and shuffling sounds. An animal smell came to my nostrils as well. The sounds became louder but they stopped well before reaching the hole. We heard a grunt and then more thumping and shuffling sounds that receded.

"An animal and a big one. It saw the light and didn't approach but it retreated instead. Curious but wary as well." Alopex spoke in a whisper.

"Not one. There are two of them." Silidora said.

Sylfan hearing is very acute and I was annoyed that Silidora could hear better under the earth than myself. I almost didn't speak up about the smell that I thought I recognized. My shame and my fear had eroded my confidence and I felt like a child among adults; what if I was wrong? That foolish stab of annoyance gave me the strength to speak up however and it was good that I did.

"Calydonian boars." I said.

"Are you sure, Breadhands?" Alopex turned to look at me and his question carried doubt.

He had accepted Silidora's estimate immediately but for me, he had his doubts. I tried to sound more confident than I really felt.

"Yes, I'm sure. The smell is unmistakable. I've been in enough hunts of such beasts to recognize it with certainty. Sometimes, calydonians wander away from Krimasand and menace our land. One of them can destroy a whole village in its rage, to say nothing of the fields they ruin."

Alopex nodded, he believed me. We waited for some time for a boar to appear below the hole but none did.

"They're not going to approach the light." Alopex said. "You know what to do." He added as he grabbed the rope and descended hand-over-hand.

As soon as he stepped on the tunnel floor, Malus threw him his spear.

"I see nothing ahead, the boars have retreated deeper down the cor-ridor. About ten metres behind me is a dead end, the tunnel stops here. I see no branching corridors."

The tiny sun hung above him and he looked at it, extended his hand and closed his fist and it was extinguished just as his fist was lit from inside. He thrust his hand before him and opened his fist and the tiny sun sped further down the tunnel, as if it had been thrown. Alopex stepped cautiously backward while describing what he saw for us. Two boars, bigger than draft horses, more massive than bears, with brown fur made of stiff bristles, regarded him with their black, beady eyes. One was a bull with huge tusks and the other a sow. Alopex retreated further down the corridor, out of our line of sight. Malus had discarded his hooded cloak and stood in his chiton, holding a spear, head down and Silidora had her bow drawn and two arrows nocked and held in the distinctive sylfan style with two more planted on the ground before her. I had a bolt nocked and steadied with a thumb, my crossbow drawn and ready to fire at a downwards angle.

Alopex continued to describe what the boars were doing but it wasn't necessary. We all heard the bull grunt, paw the ground with a front hoof and charge!

"I hate being bait!" Alopex shouted.

The ground shook from the charging, giant boar and I called to the

Gods to watch over the danaos who faced it alone and without room to maneuver. I shot the bolt and hit the boar's snout as soon as it came into my line of sight and began to reload quickly. Silidora fired two arrows, nocked two more and fired again before the boar had cleared the hole. All four struck the animal. They were easy hits, shooting at a huge target from this range but it was still an impressive feat. As soon as the boar appeared below, Malus jumped down the hole and on top of the boar's back and drove his spear so deep and with such strength that the haft broke in his hands and there wasn't much of it left. Silidora's second shot was made at the same time but no arrow struck the man of silver; one missed him by half a hand's breadth! The boar grunted in pain but it didn't break his charge and he was gone before I could reload.

"Get down there." Silidora shouted and I complied with only a momentary hesitation. If I had paused to think about it, my fear would have paralyzed me but I simply did it, riding the edge that battle brings to a man's heart. I jumped down, grabbed the rope with one hand and slid down, my leather glove protecting my palm from the abrasion. I never saw Silidora descend but she was there beside me when I reached the floor of the bottom tunnel. I think that she jumped down and landed on her feet, in full armour no less!

Alopex had flattened himself against the wall, behind a jutting, angled surface and thus had survived the boar's charge. He'd stabbed the animal with his spear as it went past him and had lost the weapon but he'd drawn his short-bladed xiphos and a double-edged dagger. As soon as the boar ran past him, he emerged from his hiding place to attack it from behind. He moved faster than any dorian I'd ever seen. He cut the tendons of the animal's back legs and it shrieked as its wounded legs buckled. It began to turn around, half-dragging its back legs and two arrows got buried in his hind-quarters. Alopex continued to stab the boar and I loosed another bolt that got buried in its chest. The bull was bleeding from a score of wounds and was frothing at the mouth. Malus was still clinging on its back, he hung on by grabbing fistfuls of bristle hairs. The man of silver struck the animal repeatedly with one fist, as he held on and blood covered his silver hand. Maddened from pain and rage, the boar shrieked, lowered its head and tried to charge again. It was a pitiful sight. I heard the twang of the bowstring and saw twin, white-feathered arrows strike both of the eyes and go deep. The bull gasped a last breath and collapsed, throwing Malus on the floor but the man of silver rose unharmed.

The sow saw her mate die and made hesitant steps back. She was afraid and reluctant to attack. She grunted and lowered her head and stamped her front legs but it was only a show to scare us.

"Take the shot, Breadhands." Alopex told me.

I drew and nocked a bolt. I shot her between the eyes but her skull was too thick. She shrieked, turned herself around and bolted down the tunnel. We followed her for some distance. The lower tunnel went on and on, like the one above but the curve was more pronounced and always inwards. At some point she stopped and stamped the ground and whined. She was afraid to go forward and as afraid to turn back and face her pursuers. We stopped and watched her fret. Finally she made up her mind. What was ahead of her held more terror than the dorians who had slain her mate. She charged us.

Alopex ran forward to meet her and I had only a moment's thought for his foolishness before I loosed a bolt and looked for a niche in the walls to avoid getting trampled. Silidora loosed three arrows at the beast. Malus simply stood and waited, his chiton in tatters but he, none the worse for wear. I saw Alopex jump to the side just before being gored and with enviable speed and skill, he buried his sword into her neck and cut down. A gout of blood fountained from the severed artery and the sow shrieked, stumbled and fell. Alopex gave her a mercy killing and the tunnel was quiet again.

Dead, the calydonian boars held much less terror than alive. I took the lantern and examined the sow.

"She's malnourished, not much fat under her fur." I said.

"She saw us slay her mate and ran from us but here, she turned around and attacked. What was she afraid of?" Silidora asked but no one could answer her.

I searched the walls and sure enough, I found chalk marks. "Dorians have followed this tunnel." I informed the rest.

"Then, they did so before the boars had the misfortune to fall down two holes or of being lured here." Malus said.

"They were starving, why then didn't they leave this place in search of food?" Alopex asked.

"Perhaps they did and there was none to be found. A good reason to stay in this section of the tunnel is the stream. Water is a more immediate need than food." I answered.

"At first it would be so but afterwards, when hunger began to gnaw on their insides, they should have gone in search of food." Alopex insisted.

Silidora answered, "It was what you think it was Alopex. Fear. Neither food nor water kept them here - fear did. Fear made the sow turn around and attack."

"Then, we shouldn't rest before seeing for ourselves what a calydonian boar was afraid of." Alopex commented.

He gestured and the tiny sun sped further down the tunnel. There was no disagreement so we went back to fetch our gear and we resumed the exploration.

We didn't go far, only a few minutes' walk. I was the first who saw it.

"There's a side corridor ahead of us, it branches to the right. There's something on the wall there." I wasn't sure what it was but the sight of it made me shiver involuntarily.

"I...see it." Silidora said but she didn't add more detail and there was hesitation in her voice.

I felt drawn towards that thing on the wall as much as I was repelled by it. All of us slowed our step. Cold sweat trickled down my spine and I wanted to turn back. Inwardly I cursed myself for being a coward.

"Move. We're stronger than this." The brother-king's voice was gruff and sounded as if he was forcing the words out of his lips.

We went on, our steps heavy and slow. I followed the questors and held my pride before me like the proverbial carrot but what I really wanted to do, was to run back and never come this way again. My palms were slick from sweat and I wiped them on my jerkin often to retain a good grip on my crossbow. We went closer, ever more reluctantly.

I'd seen it first and thus, I was the first to suffer. Broken bones of every kind were driven into the wall and arranged in a crude depiction of a chalyvos with the head of a boar. It was like a painting, made with the bones of dorians and I felt nauseous at the sight of it. All who saw it felt revulsion and tried to avert their gaze but the bone painting drew all eyes and held them fast. Heads turned away, only to slowly turn towards it again. We were disgusted and mesmerized at the same time.

There was a sharp pain behind my eyes and I cried out, dropped my crossbow and covered my eyes. The bone-thing appeared then. We heard it coming from the tunnel opening to our right. A sound of rhythmic grinding and sounds of breaking, the sound one hears inside him when he breaks a bone, magnified a hundredfold. The pain passed and I opened my eyes to see. The bone-thing was made in the semblance of a dorian, a crude imitation of a chalyvos, made with bones of all kinds. Its movement was jerky and the bones that made it grounded against each other and some would break with every step but held together somehow. I knew then that it was a crude copy of me because I had laid eyes first on the bone painting. I knew that this *Bone Semblance* was coming to kill me.

I was paralyzed with horror and revulsion but the questors weren't so severely affected. Silidora loosed an arrow that she'd held ready and then put the bow down and drew her magnificent sword. Alopex, armed with Silidora's spear, ran towards the Semblance, stepped on the right wall – he actually ran two steps on the wall - and leaped behind it as Malus confronted it head-on. The man of silver began to hammer the foe with his fists as Alopex struck from behind. Silidora entered the fray with her leafblade, wielded with both hands. The Semblance fought with bony spikes that protruded from its arms and with claws and even with tusks that it somehow formed from the bones comprising its body. The questors fought with maniacal fury, turning their revulsion into anger. I shook my fugue and was the last to enter the fray and it was only then, when I struck the Semblance with my hammer, shattering one of its leg bones, that it produced a sound, an ugly, high-pitched cry that was blessedly short. We shattered that unholy thing into pieces but that wasn't a true victory, not really. When it was shattered into fragments of bone, that semblance of myself took with it a piece of me, a part of my sanity. I lost all sense and collapsed.

I awoke disoriented and drenched in sweat. I didn't know where I was and I called Lorna's name. My voice was feeble. They gave me water. I remembered vividly a nightmare of running down tunnels of bone that had eyes everywhere, cruel, unnatural eyes, watching me. I was headed towards the center of a descending, spiral tunnel - the very heart of this unnatural place. I didn't want to but I didn't have a choice. I had a boar's head. The others were talking to me but reality and the nightmare blurred together and I was confused.

The questors had carried me further down the branching tunnel, past the bone painting. They'd halted a good distance away, out of sight of it. They were exhausted and had to rest. The questors kept watch with shifts and denied my offer to take a turn. That should have insulted me, should have prodded me to stubborn pride but I let it be. My head was filled with wool and clear thinking as well as the mustering of the will to do anything was so very difficult. Alopex was very worried about me. He asked me many questions and fussed over me but I remember little. I went to sleep again but I didn't sleep well.

When I awoke, I was feeling better. At least my mind had cleared and I felt rested. I ate without appetite. I felt the change within me but it was knowledge that couldn't be put into words and couldn't be shared. A seed had been planted inside of me, a seed of madness. It made me sick but I didn't want to think about it. Thought flowed like water around it and I couldn't focus on what it was that I knew, so I reasoned it away. Silidora showed me a script on the wall, made with chalk. The writing was in the golden tongue and it said, *'They're all mad. I'll try to get past the bone painting, go home. Jader Bluehammer.'* I shuddered as I imagined Jader looking upon the bone painting again and fighting the bone semblance alone.

"Did you know him?" Silidora asked me. She didn't need me to read it to her.

"I did. A good man, one of the first to enter these tunnels."

Alopex wanted to know what dreams we had. All of them had nightmares of one kind or another, just like me. Silidora asked the king what he dreamed about and he said that his dream was about a child's rhyme, one that girls in the Hold had been singing before we'd left; a song that counted a Panoptis' eyes. None of the others remembered such a thing.

"You were there too Malus, the girls that were jumping the rope and were rhyming, 'the first eye, it will make you lie, the second eye it will make you cry...' and so on. Surely you remember."

"I don't." Malus stated.

Alopex frowned but he didn't insist. Silidora had a nightmare of a black void that swallowed the sky, a void that hungered and devoured the stars and the sun. Malus only said that he'd dreamed of what he had lost and only Alopex understood I think. I said nothing and the questors let me keep my peace.

Silidora asked me as we made ready to continue, "Rathi, if we had to go back and get past the bone painting, would you do it?"

I went white as a sheet at the suggestion. The thought of going back and seeing that painting again filled me with dread. I admitted as much.

"Fortunately Breadhands, you won't have to." Alopex said. "We shall go forward, find the spawn of the Dark Host and take its unholy life. The battle has begun between us. The Panoptis seeks to erode our sanity and our resolve. It is a sly and evil creature but we are stronger and we will endure. Have faith, for the Gods are with us."

The brother-king's voice held only determination and conviction without the slightest hint of fear. In that moment, he didn't seem as young as I'd thought he was. Inwardly, I wished that I had his courage.

I would follow the questors as I had pledged to do but from that point on, my terror of going back robbed me of the heroism of going forward.

We resumed our exploration. The new tunnel was much the same as those we'd previously travelled and it also had an inward curve, more pronounced than the one of the tunnel above but similar to the curve of the tunnel that we'd left behind. After about two hours walk, we found wild dogs - three of them. They had no eyes, just empty holes. Two of the animals just stood close together, their tongues sticking out. The third was lying down, barely breathing. There were hardly any droppings and no smell of urine in their section of the tunnel. They were unresponsive to anything we did. Silidora tried to give them water but they didn't drink. They were just standing there, waiting to die. Why would any creature do that? Were they food for the darkcild or was their suffering a source of amusement, an act of cruelty? We couldn't leave the poor animals in such misery. We killed them before continuing down the mismatched tunnel. They made no sound. I followed the questors deeper into the nightmare.

At the end of the tunnel, we found another hole that led to another tunnel running below us at an angle. We descended deeper into that purposeless network of empty corridors. Nothing barred our way and nothing changed in the construction and feel of the deeper tunnel. We walked on, the tiny sun was replaced by the sylfaea's light sparrow again. The single lit lantern bobbed above me and in front of me. I walked on as if in a dream. I stopped taking notice of my surroundings; I stopped looking for the chalk markings left behind by men and women who had died in there. I'm sorry to say I didn't care enough.

Silidora was the first to notice it from afar. She gasped softly and halted after catching just the barest glimpse of it. Malus and Alopex halted as well but I went forward a few steps more, oblivious to the others halting, until I too saw it. It was the same as before, about a hundred strides ahead, bones set into the wall opposite a branching tunnel. An intersection guarded by another bone painting. I averted my gaze immediately.

"Only one." Alopex said, his meaning clear. "Whatever happens, let it happen to only one of us. Should a bone semblance appear, like before, the rest join the battle. I'll go."

There was no argument from the other questors. I don't think the others were afraid, or unwilling to face danger. They were simply too practical to argue Alopex's decision without a good reason. Also, both Malus and the Maiden of Mereandil valued his judgment and decisions above their own. Even if he was never named as such, the fox-named king was the leader of our band. The others drew weapons, nocked arrows and made ready. As Alopex walked with slow steps, the thought occurred to me that like Silidora, he was an adept of the Orphic Secrets and a man of skill and courage. If he was to save my family and my polis, he should be spared this madness that had afflicted me. He hadn't yet seen it – he needed light for that and the bone painting was still too far away. If a seed of madness took root within Alopex, all would be lost.

I could think clear enough at that moment to make that decision. That was my moment of courage and greatness. I had joined the questors to wash away my shame and die, for them and for my polis.

I ran.

They shouted my name and they came after me but they couldn't stop me from being the one to view the painting first.

It was hideous and obscene. The bones were all taken from dorians. Some were yellowed, some were gnawed and the marrow was licked clean. The painting depicted three little chalyvan girls, one was jumping a rope held by the other two. Their arms and legs were tentacles and each tentacle ended in an eye. I despaired then because I remembered that this was Alopex's nightmare. Had I failed? Did Alopex's decision to view the painting somehow counted above the act of actually viewing it? I felt needles being driven into my eyes and I screamed. After that, they came with a sickening sound of bones crunching, grinding and breaking.

There were four Bone Semblances this time. All were jerky, horrible collections of bones that resembled a chalyvos. I was glad and I must have laughed because I hadn't failed after all; the bone painting had spawned these monstrosities in the image of the one who had viewed it. A seed was already within me and so there were more semblances and they were stronger. I cared not at all for them, only for the fact that my sacrifice hadn't been in vain. I laughed with relief and I wailed from despair and I waited to die.

A gust of wind howled with fury down the corridor and threw me down on the floor. I felt the wind like a giant hand that pressed against me but I was the least affected because I was protected from the full force of the gale by the windcaller. Silidora had sent the mystical wind to protect me. The bone things - all four of them - were picked up by that wind and thrown back against the walls and were blown down the tunnel. When the wind died out however, the pieces gathered, the Bone Semblances reassembled themselves and came on again. They were cracked and parts of them were missing, broken by the impact with walls and floor but all four were still moving. The questors carried me back and made their stand away from the horrid painting. When the Semblances reached me, the questors were before me, to do battle on my behalf.

I didn't fight because I was too weak to even lift my hammer or my crossbow. In any case, the three didn't need my help. They were a whirlwind of destruction among the enemies. They met bone spikes and claws with bronze and steel and they countered bone fangs and tusks with magic and skill unmatched. They suffered wounds but none was serious and they let no Semblance strike me.

Their victory was hard-earned but for me, it was hollow. The Bone Semblances didn't need to strike me physically because at the moment of their destruction, I felt more seeds being planted inside me. The seed that I already carried, cracked open and madness leaked out like puss.

I knew then that my eyes had ceased to be my own ever since the first seed of madness had taken root. The Panoptis had taken my sight for his own and had been looking out of my eyes, all this time. The madness that was drowning my thoughts under a nightmare tide wasn't born in my psyche - *it was Panoptis' own*. Just as the darkcild was in my thoughts and looked out of my eyes, so too I was in his own thoughts and looked out of his own eyes. So many images, confusion and chaos, vile thoughts and a dozen skewed views of a house of madness. I was just a mortal while he was a Nightson of a Dark Goddess and a Gigas. I was small and naked before his terrible might. He laughed at me and I howled from despair as my mind's eye opened by force. He showed me everything because it amused him to torment me with knowledge of doom and with the horror that was waiting in the dark.

We were the last. I saw all those who had gone before us. I saw them stumble through the tunnels, I saw them suffer and die. I saw the hero of my clan, Lothi Bronzehand, lose heart! I saw him flee from the sight of yet another bone painting in his exploration of the tunnels. Half his companions went forward but he went back and many followed him. When the Panoptis found him, Lothi fought bravely but he died a coward nonetheless. Nothing remained of him, of any of them, as nothing would remain of us. Only one had been allowed to escape, in order to bring more with his tales and with the false hope that if one could escape and return, others could as well.

The Nightson was the Eye of Death and he would snuff out our lives like candle flames. He would confront us when we were already beaten and he would slay us and take our flesh and our bones and our eyes to complete his Mother's house. She would be born into the Earth and reside in the house he had made for her and spawn more darkcildra. This would become a hive of Panoptes that would bring ruin and death to all in my polis, to the land and beyond. We were trapped inside a *spiral labyrinth of madness* that led down, down, down to a pit of doom and there was no way out and no way back.

I was lost for a long time after the four bone semblances were shattered. The questors tried to help me but after a time they ceased trying to bring me to my senses. They only bore witness to the ravings of a madman, heard the disjointed accounts of the ordeals and the final battles of all those who had died in there and of the Panoptis' work and purpose.

Alopex listened carefully and he alone fully understood what awaited us. It was given to him as a mystic devoted to Hermes, the Messenger of the Gods and the walker of all roads, to know the road, the destination, the distance. Under the earth, everything was different of course and the tunnels we walked shouldn't constitute a true road. Yet, they did. In a sense that he couldn't understand till then, we walked a road...that led nowhere. He'd known that it led down, deeper into the earth but that wasn't the true destination of that road. The distance was unknowable as well, sometimes finite and others infinite but always unknown. He listened closely to my ravings and his own knowledge was put into context and he understood.

After the Panoptis had amused itself enough, he closed my mind's eye and somehow made me ignore the gravity of all that he had shown me. I knew but I couldn't associate that knowledge with importance, couldn't attach feelings to all that awaited me, us and the Hold. When I'd recovered enough to walk, we continued the exploration. The other questors told me nothing of my ravings and of the revelations that they had heard. You see, I had said that the Panoptis could see them through my eyes and they had to assume that the darkcild could also hear them. So, they kept silent.

After a few hours of walking down that tunnel, we stopped to rest. That would be our second night in the tunnels. The next day we'd go deeper and find a third bone painting which would spawn a dozen bone semblances but I didn't care enough to inform the others of that fact. I ate mechanically and paid no mind to anyone else. When I finally fell into a troubled sleep, the questors left me and went a good distance away to hold council in whispers.

"We must either kill him or at least bind him and leave him behind. The enemy cannot be allowed to spy on us any longer." Malus said and I cannot fault him. What was a dorian to one such as he? A dorian subverted by the enemy no less.

"This isn't the first time we have to deal with enemy awareness through one of our own. Rathi put himself in much danger for us. It's a poor way to repay such bravery." Silidora said and I wish I had heard her speak those words.

"Breadhands isn't our problem. What happened to him will also happen to us before long. Surely, more bone paintings await us deeper into these tunnels." Alopex said.

"What do you propose then?" Malus asked.

"We all heard Rathi's ravings. We cannot continue like this. I'm convinced that we'll find more bone paintings and that more of us will be afflicted with this madness that consumes the chalyvos. If we continue, we'll lose our grip on sanity and probably split up and the Panoptis will come to slay us at his leisure. From Rathi's ravings, that's how the Nightson dealt with Bronzehand's group. So, I say that we force a confrontation!"

Alopex was wild-eyed, his movements were exaggerated and sweat plastered his hair to his forehead and neck. He knew and so he was afraid - afraid of the enclosed space and of the pressure of the earth above him, afraid of the darkness and of the doom that awaited him. Most of all, he was afraid of a future in which we would fail. The other questors heard his suspicions and felt the same urgency, the same need to avert their doom but it's different to feel than it is to know. A strong feeling consumes you but it's fleeting and it allows you to doubt its truth and sooner or later, it fades. Knowledge on the other hand is truth and it permits you no lies, no joy and it never ends. Alopex had pieced together the knowledge but wisely he kept most of it to himself.

Silidora spoke, "I don't see how we can do what you suggest. The Panoptis waits for us at the heart of this dungeon, where he builds his mother's house. Only there can we force him to fight and it seems that we cannot reach it with our sanity intact."

"This isn't a dungeon of random tunnels. This is a labyrinth; a spiral labyrinth which was made to house a vast darkness. There is only one way and it leads to the bottom of the pit. All others who came before us suffered the same fate - some went mad, some turned back and all of them were finally slain by the Panoptis when they were at their weakest. Don't you see?"

"No Alopex, I don't see the significance of what you say."

The Maiden of Mereandil was becoming doubtful of Alopex's judgment and perhaps his sanity as well and that was dangerous. If the questors stopped trusting each other, all would be lost.

"Rathi never spoke of a madman going back. In his disjointed accounts of all those who died in here, the madmen always went forward. Only the cowards went back and they were still mostly sane, yet unaffected by the bone paintings. Also, think of the final battle of his kinsman. The Panoptis came for him only after Lothi turned back." Alopex was desperate to make them understand.

"Are you saying that we can force a confrontation by turning back?" Malus asked.

"Yes my friend. The darkcild is in no hurry. While he waits, his foes fall under the madness of the bone paintings and they suffer wounds and exhaustion by fighting bone semblances of themselves. And with each step, madness claims them. Most of them have died on the way to the heart of the labyrinth. I don't think that any dorian has ever reached it. Only when they turn back, does the Panoptis seek them and kills them."

Silidora wasn't convinced, "This plan of yours entails us encountering one or both bone paintings again, while the heart of the labyrinth could be under the next hole we find or at the end of this tunnel. There haven't been any chalk markings for some time now, in case you haven't noticed. No one has reached this far before us. Your plan will cost us needless confrontation with bone semblances and the insanity and weakness with which the bone paintings affect the viewers. It will cost us time and that is a luxury that we can ill-afford. Ultimately, it may rob us of victory. Lastly, your plan is founded on the ravings of a madman."

Always, the Maiden was the one to prod them onwards, the one to rue every minute lost. She had no fear other than the fear of failure and defeat and she was on another quest, bigger than the one that she pursued in the Panoptis' labyrinth. That was her failing I think, to always think ahead and lose the moment. However, none could fault her logic.

"We can do nothing for Androktetes if we're dead. Die here and all hope is lost with you, with us. I see everything clearly and I know that I am in the right and if you do not do as I say, we'll all perish." Alopex said, not without anger.

"What about Rathi then? If you're right, he'll refuse to go back. He wouldn't hear of it when I asked him about such a course earlier so in that you must be right. He'll die alone in the dark if we leave him. Are you prepared to sacrifice him to test your theory or do you propose to carry him with us bound and helpless?"

"You forget, I think that the chalyvos came here to die so that we can defeat the Panoptis. In any case, worry not for him. I will take care of Breadhands and in doing so, I intend to mislead our enemy. We need every advantage we can get. Are you with me Silidora Windwhisper? This I must know now."

Silidora was skeptical and like all sylfaen, slow to really trust any dorian that wasn't *Foamborn,* like her timeless race. It was one thing to trust a comrade-in-arms, even to value his judgment and quite another to gamble everything on his interpretation of a madman's ravings. The brother-king was a gambler and sometimes he was a fool and he had only lived a brief, danaan lifetime. Silidora had walked the Earth for two hundred years and she had never been a fool. The Panoptis could be just a day's walk away without any other bone paintings to bar their way. He could even be one hour's walk from them. None had reached this far before them. She gave the whole matter a lot of thought before giving her answer.

Alopex didn't need to ask the man of silver whether he would follow him or not. They were family - brothers not by blood but by love. They talked some more but there was not a lot to say after Silidora had spoken. They returned to where I was fast asleep and they rested.

I woke up screaming and Malus, who was shaking me, regarded me with a frown on his perfect face. The nightmare was so vivid that I had much difficulty in connecting to my surroundings and those who were with me. Reality had ceased being real for me.

"I know why we haven't found any corpses of all those who died in here, no remains, no flesh, no bones." I said.

"We know Rathi, you told us yesterday what the Panoptis does with the remains of all those he has killed." Alopex remarked.

"I did? I don't remember...He waits and he hates you Alopex most of all, oh, how he hates you. I think he will kill you last."

Alopex said nothing, he just looked at me with pity. He looked young and vibrant while I felt wretched and old. He held a water-flask, it was half-empty. I asked for it to wet my throat but he drew it back.

"Not yet Rathi but soon. You've forgotten your own water-flask, there to your right. Drink and have something to eat, we must get going. This is our last day in this spiral labyrinth. You will need your strength." Alopex said.

It took me a while to think on what the brother-king had said and I began to laugh, without mirth. My laughter turned to tears soon enough and I told them, "Don't think questors that I don't know what has befallen me. I know that I'm useless to you and I know that I am doomed. This is the last day you say? Perhaps. Ever since we entered here, we've been living our last days. There's no hope for us, no hope..."

I was pathetic. I was terrified and lost. I was mad. The Eye of Death tormented me with his vile thoughts that burrowed into my mind like whispering worms. He gave me no reprieve.

"I have heard enough. It's obvious that our quest must end if we value our lives. I refuse to die here in the company of a sniveling danaos and a half-mad chalyvos. I'm going back." Silidora stated in anger.

No one said anything and I was too stupid then and stunned by her statement besides, to realize the gravity of the situation. The sylfaea shouldered her pack and with bow in hand, left us. She went in the dark, without any light. Didn't she need light? Were there stars in here that I couldn't see? A few heartbeats later, I couldn't hear her footfalls.

"I will not go back." I told the talls.

I was more afraid to go back than to go forward and I knew not why such a cold fear gripped my heart every time I thought of viewing again the two bone paintings.

"You won't have to, Breadhands. The three of us are going to finish this quest." Alopex said.

I ate nothing and got ready. I had no appetite, no hunger. I remembered the animals, the boars and the dogs. In the end, that would be me, if the Panoptis didn't kill me outright. I couldn't summon enough energy to care about my fate however. I quenched my thirst, shouldered my pack and nocked a bolt to my crossbow with trembling hands. I began walking but Alopex put his hand on my shoulder.

"That's the way back to the skin, the way Silidora went. Do you want to follow her out of here Rathi? I thought that you entered the labyrinth to become a hero of your people."

I was confused for a moment but Alopex was right and I let him lead me forward, towards my doom.

So, the three of us started on the last leg of delving in those tunnels. I was looking back often, in the hope of seeing Silidora return to us but she didn't. Alopex's tiny sun lighted our way and he kept the mystical light close. He too was afraid and I thought that he too must have carried a seed of madness. Why else would any man want to go forward and not turn back? Silidora was the only one of us who was sane and that was why she had fled. It was always thus with all those who had come before.

The shadows were sinister, the silence was ominous and the tunnel seemed sometimes to shrink, others to enlarge. Was the tunnel around me pulsating, like a vein or was it my imagination? I was drenched in sweat after only an hour's walk. I enjoyed a small mercy when, a little while after we began walking, the voice and the thoughts of the monster ceased to burrow into my mind. I was numb with a cold fear but at least I was free of the burrowing worms of the darkcild's madness and malice.

I was the last to see it and the only one of us that was surprised. It was perhaps thirty strides ahead when I raised my head and looked at it and the sight of it made me fall on my knees, my legs too weak to support me. Ahead of me was a bone painting, three chalyvan girls, one jumping the rope the other two were swinging, tentacles and eyes. I had been led back, not forward. I began to scream and I fired my crossbow at the painting. Malus grabbed me from behind and lifted me up in a bear hug. I struggled briefly but the man of silver was too strong. Alopex made me drink from his water-flask. There was magic in that clear water and it burned down my throat like saltwater forced down a drowning man's mouth as he gasps for air. I panicked and struggled but soon the water washed away the confusion from my mind and the exhaustion from my body. I felt renewed. I felt strong and whole after being weak and fragmented for what seemed like days and nights uncounted. I sighed and asked to be let down. Malus released me. The seeds were still inside me but the madness had been pushed back and I could control my fear. I had my dignity back and I could die like a man instead of like a dumb animal which was what the Panoptis had reduced me to.

"Breadhands, arm yourself and get ready for battle." Alopex told me with a voice that conveyed urgency.

"I know that he's coming Alopex and thanks to you I'm ready. Tell me this, how did we turn back and what did you give me to drink?"

"Unlike you chalyvos, I did not rest. I communed with the Gods and prepared the healing draught that I gave you. Some of your ills were within my power to heal and the Panoptis' influence is buried for now. It is not gone because not even the Gods can cure a man of madness. That is something that only you can do for yourself. Nevertheless, I've given you the time you need to do what you came here for. As for how we turned back, I gave you a lie that you could believe despite your best judgement. Prepare yourself, If I'm right, battle is at hand."

I felt it then, a madness overtaking me, a pressure building behind my eyes and I wanted to shut them, to deny myself the sight of him. My voice trembled and my heart skipped a beat as I said, "He is here."

"Will you put me to sleep with your lyre, like your God did to my father?" The strong voice resounded ahead of us, a mocking voice, the voice that had been whispering madness and horror in my head.

The Nightson appeared at the intersection ahead. He came from the right tunnel and stood there, framed by the bone painting behind him. He was very tall and naked, powerfully built with bone-white skin, totally hairless. His odor was strong and foul. His mouth was too wide, it split his head in two and he had a mocking smile that revealed yellowed and blackened teeth. He resembled a danaos more than any other human but he had no genitalia, he was a genderless creature that only mimicked a man. His whole body was covered with eyes, some bigger than others. Even his limbs and his head were covered with eyes. Some were closed but most were open. The biggest eye of all was on his chest and it was closed, with a disgusting milky-yellow crust on the lid and at the edges. He was a sickening sight but I had been afraid for so long that when I saw him, there was relief mixed with my fear and disgust. Here was the foe at last!

I let a bolt fly and his left arm shot forward, palm open. The eye on his palm closed and my bolt disappeared before it even reached him! It was like all the stories said, each eye that closed unmade anything that it saw last. That eye wouldn't open again until the Panoptis slept or else what was unmade would be real again and he would be struck by my bolt. That was small consolation however, since he had so many eyes. Alopex answered the darkcild in that amused and confident voice of his.

"I expected you to be ready for such a ploy. Also, I don't have a lyre. Perhaps your father can play for you in the Pits of Tartaros, where I will send you!" Then the danaos turned to me and he shouted, *"Rathi, run!"*

Alopex and Malus turned and fled and it took me a moment to overcome my surprise and follow them.

Our light, the tiny sun, was left behind and it was snuffed out, unmade by an eye that had closed. Even mystical wonders couldn't endure a Panoptis' gaze. Alopex had a lighted lantern in hand and by its feeble light, he and Malus avoided stumbling on the uneven ground.

The darkcild didn't pursue us. He simply walked after us and shouted, *"Run like cowards, run like frightened animals, run deeper into my House. There is no escape!"*

The Panoptis' cruel laughter reverberated in the tunnel, the sound deep and inhuman.

We didn't run far before Alopex stopped and said that this is far enough. I didn't ask why we ran away and why we stopped where we did. I got busy winding my crossbow as I caught my breath. Alopex invoked the Sun God and another tiny sun was born which he placed inside a depression in the wall. It shed enough ambient light to dispel the darkness but it couldn't be seen to be unmade from afar. The Panoptis was coming, I saw him while he was still in the darkened part of the corridor. I warned the questors and I shot again. Another eye closed and I frantically reloaded. Alopex and Malus lighted all of our lanterns and left them on the floor. Alopex held our last spear - it was Silidora's spear and I briefly wondered why she'd left it behind - and his free hand was on Malus' shoulder. The priest invoked the Messenger but I couldn't hear what he asked for because my blood was pounding inside my head. My terror made me fumble with my weapon.

"I will crush your skulls and break your bones. I will use your remains to build my Mother's House but your hearts - those I shall devour." The Panoptis shouted as he picked up the pace.

He was eager to kill. An invocation to the Crippled Smith came unbidden to my lips as I fired again, just as the Nightson entered the light. My bolt winked out of existence. The Panoptis halted then and his eyes regarded me; so many eyes, angry, bloodshot and merciless. One of them closed and my crossbow was no longer in my hands. More of them closed and my hammer, my breastplate and helmet were unmade and blinked out of existence. I stood unarmoured and unarmed against the enemy. Another eye closed and I felt my skin being ripped open on my face; warm blood gushed out. I screamed as my flesh was unmade. Then, the eyes turned as one to regard Alopex. He was the object of the darkcild's hatred more than any of us.

The king stood bravely before the Panoptis, only ten strides between them and he said to Malus, "Godspeed my friend," as he hefted the spear and threw.

Arrows whistled above my head while the spear was still in the air and Malus broke into a run towards the Panoptis. I saw him run impossibly fast and I heard no footfalls because his feet weren't touching the ground! Eyes closed and the spear, as well as the arrows, were unmade.

I heard the sylfaea curse behind me because she lost her bow to an eye and I saw her draw a knife. Where had she come from? She ran past me and went forward to meet the monster. Alopex drew his bronze knives and began throwing them with such speed and skill that I hadn't witnessed before. Malus ran past the Panoptis and the monster was either too distracted or too indifferent towards a foe that sought to avoid him and flee, instead of attacking him. Was he fleeing, though? Surely not. There was a plan of battle being unveiled that I knew naught of and that was good. If I had known, the Panoptis would have known as well.

I had no weapons, so I grabbed two bolts out of my quiver and ran at the monster, half-blinded from the blood on my face, shouting, "For Glistenwall!"

The darkspawn didn't even bother to unmake the bolts I held, as I had hoped. I only wanted to close some more of his eyes, give the questors a distraction they could use, give them a fighting chance. As I ran past Silidora, who retreated from the monster, weaponless, I didn't see her magnificent sword. It was unmade then. I had such hopes that *Defender* would prove to be the monster's doom but they'd been for naught. I went at him and the Panoptis simply kicked me away. The damn monster was so tall that I only reached up to his waist and his strength was incredible. I was thrown back, stunned by the force of the blow but I left both bolts nailed into the meat of his foreleg. His blood was green. I saw two eyes on his leg close and the bolts disappear and I smiled as I struggled to stand up. The Panoptis screamed in pain as a bronze knife struck him on his right arm, piercing an eye. It was unmade an eye-blink later. The foe was wounded but we had to do better than that.

"Good throw Alopex, a few more and the bastard is done for!" I shouted for encouragement.

"That was my last, if you must know." Alopex's comment dampened my joy for our small victory.

"This is the last of *everything* for you. You think that your petty deceptions, the sylfaea's cowardice and your turning back, have given you an advantage? *You will die* like all the rest and after you, all the people of this land will either die or become Mother's slaves."

The Panoptis in his anger rushed us, intending to snuff out our lives with his fists. As he did so, eyes closed and the flesh ripped open on all three of us. Jagged wounds appeared on arms and legs, chest and face and red blood painted all of us. I had the worst of it because the questors were still protected by their armour and flesh unseen could not be unmade. I was glad for my pain and I wouldn't have it any other way - that was what I was there for. My hate for the Panoptis gave me the strength to withstand the suffering of my many wounds. I palmed two more bolts and got in his way – that much I could do.

The sylfaea raised her voice in song despite her own pain and she moved her arms in a spiral pattern. Winds blew in the tunnel, they blew towards her from every direction and she wove them into one powerful gust, into a battering ram made of raging wind that she sent with a thrusting motion to meet the charging darkcild. I saw eyes close in succession, four I think or five and heard the wind dying abruptly. One moment it was roaring deafeningly towards the darkspawn and the next there wasn't even a breeze to mark the magic's death. I threw myself on his wounded leg, tried to trip him or slow him down. I nailed more bolts on his leg with all my strength. He grabbed me and lifted me from the ground with one hand and threw me against a wall. I struck the stone and passed out.

Alopex and Silidora fought with the monster from opposite sides and when one distracted the foe, the other struck. The king depended upon his agility to evade the powerful blows of his foe while the sylfaea was protected by fierce winds that turned away the monster's fists. They fought with whatever weapons remained to them and when those were gone, they fought with their fists. The sylfaea drove her last knife into an eye at the side of his midsection and Alopex gouged out an eye on the Panoptis' backside with his hands.

The Panoptis' scream of rage brought me to my senses with a jolt, because his hate reverberated in my mind. I opened my eyes to see the armours of the questors being unmade. The beautiful promethean armour was no more, its reality was devoured by seven eyes or more and Silidora's protective winds were also gone, her magic unmade. The Panoptis had almost reached his limit, most of the eyes I could see were closed. However, his monstrous strength and endurance were enough to beat the life out of the brave warriors who faced him still, unarmed and injured, their flesh flayed and torn.

The Eye of Death struck Alopex a mighty blow and then he grabbed the sylfaea by the throat. I tried to get up but I couldn't do it. I was bleeding from a dozen wounds and my back hurt terribly; every movement was agony. Silidora was lifted in the air and I heard her choking. She struggled futilely. My first thought was of the man of silver - where was he? A moment later I remembered that he'd fled. Fortunately, Alopex recovered quickly and lost no time. He had tied his xiphos on his back and had covered it cunningly. Now he brought the sheath to his front and grabbed the hilt. He attacked the monster from behind - not that it mattered, the Panoptis could see everywhere at once - but he kept his scabbarded sword concealed by his body until the last second. With terrific speed he drew and lunged before the Panoptis could un-make the weapon.

Alopex stabbed the Panoptis on his lower back and drove the blade deep before it was unmade. Green blood gushed from the wound and the darkcild screamed in pain and turned to face the brother-king, let-ting the sylfaea fall on the floor. He tried to grab Alopex who was again swifter than his opponent. Despite his wounds, the Panoptis was nei-ther slowed nor weakened however, not that I could see. Alopex was wounded and tired; he couldn't keep avoiding the monster for much longer.

"*Malus!*" The brother-king screamed and I pitied him for his broth-er's betrayal, for I thought then that his desperate cry for help would go unanswered. But the earth trembled, the walls vibrated and I heard the scraping of metal on stone coming from the darkness of the corridor be-yond, down which Malus had fled. A grunt of pain, one of such volume that it couldn't have been issued by a dorian throat, filled the tunnel. The Panoptis ceased his attack upon Alopex and made a few steps to-wards that sound. The king seized the opportunity to go to the sylfaea's side. And then I saw him - the Silver Dragon!

His bulk filled the tunnel and he moved with difficulty, with each step his body scraped along the wall and the ceiling. Chunks of stone were broken and dust filled the tunnel. His wings were folded but they snagged on the uneven surfaces and the jutting planes of the tunnel. The dragon's face bore a grimace of pain. I searched that face for a resemblance, for some common features to confirm my suspicion but really – who else could it be? I beheld Malus Argent, in his true form.

Alopex's voice was triumphant as he shouted, *"The bastard of Argos is ready for you Malus. Most of his eyes are closed and spent and he has to choose which direction to face."*

Somehow, I found the strength to stand and walk and I joined the two questors with a slow and painful half-crawl. The effort made me spit blood and the sharp pain told me that I had at least one broken rib and a pierced lung. The coming of the dragon gave pause to the Panop-tis and gave us some time to recover our wits. The Nightson just stood there, facing us but really looking at the dragon with the many eyes on the back of his body. Only two eyes were still open at the front side of his body, some more at the back. He smiled cruelly and it gave me shivers. The sylfaea was bleeding from a dozen wounds all over her body and her neck was purple. Only Alopex was in good shape still, I guess the Panoptis saved him for last.

"Can you fight?" Alopex asked Silidora.

"Are you strong enough to do as you said? Then you'll see if I can still fight. Otherwise it won't matter one way or the other." She answered with a scratchy voice from her bruised throat.

They didn't ask me how I was - it was obvious. I was a mass of torn flesh and blood, my breaths were shallow and fast and my suffering was written on what remained of my face. I couldn't fight. My thoughts could barely penetrate the haze of my pain. I settled with my back to the wall and watched the confrontation of Panoptis and Dragon. I so hoped that it was over now, that the silver dragon would grab the darkcild in its jaws and take his cursed life.

"You shall pay for the pain of this crawl through your tunnels and for my injured wings." Malus said in a heavy, inhuman voice and lunged forward.

He was slow because he had to tear up the whole tunnel for each stride he took. The Panoptis wasn't moving however. He just stood and waited and finally turned to face the dragon.

"Pathetic dorians, I wanted to use my hands to take your lives but you have proven tiresome. Your ploy was good enough but you haven't known one such as me before. *I am the consort of my Mother and mine are the Eyes of Death. Gaze upon your doom.*"

Malus hadn't yet reached him and he frantically tried to move faster as he shouted, *"The eye Alopex, the largest of all, it is opening!"*

The Eye of Death, as crazy Hojar had said. It was the one on his chest - it almost covered his whole chest - and it was opening to unmake the dragon's life. Even though I wasn't in that eye's field of vision, I wanted to crawl as far away from that terrible orb as I could and not even the pain of my wounds could stop me. What could Alopex do against that?

I had my answer a moment later as the chosen of the Gods raised his hands and his face to the ceiling, as if he could pierce the stone and the earth to look at the open sky.

"Ares, hear me!" Alopex shouted. *"The land sings of your victory over the Titan, Opladamos. I claim the echo of your victory, I claim the memory of the slaying, I claim the name of your triumph."*

His words reverberated painfully in my ears. The temperature dropped abruptly. For me, it was all done in the space of a heartbeat or two but for the chosen one it was different. At the moment of invocation, he left the mortal plane and knelt on the shore of the River of Faith and there he was tested by the God of War. He never spoke to me of those tests but he was found worthy, else you wouldn't be reading this tale. He returned to us bearing a *Miracle*.

Inky blackness filled the priest's hands, expanded, elongated and coalesced into a spear that seemed to draw the light and to trail smoke made of shadow. On his face, I could see the pain and ecstasy of the divine power that he held. The hand that held the spear blackened and his face contorted in pain as he got ready to throw.

"*Alopex!*" Malus cried and my attention turned back to the Panoptis and the dragon.

I saw the entire upper half of the Panoptis' back break open. A horizontal slash appeared and I thought that it was a wound because green blood gushed out and ran down his body, to make the few eyes that were still open, blink and close. Then the slash grew larger and I felt a pain in my chest, sharp and biting. I felt a cold hand squeeze my heart and my lungs wouldn't draw breath. I had a moment of clarity then and I remembered that the Panoptis had spoken in plural; he had said '*Mine are the Eyes of Death.*'

Alopex understood what he was seeing and his moment of triumph turned to black despair. All of the lesser eyes of the Panoptis closed as the two larger eyes, one on his chest and one on his back, opened fully to gaze upon us all. The darkspawn laughed. Alopex held the power to deny the Panoptis' eye of death. That was his plan all along - that was to be the climax of the battle and our victory blow.

However, it was not to be.

Alopex had the power to deny one eye of death, not two. He had to choose who would live and who would die. With a cry of regret and with tears flowing down his cheeks, he threw the black spear. The eye of death that beheld the three of us, was struck. It was struck by the memory of a Titan's death and it proved to be too much. The eye blackened and shriveled and became ash that flaked away, leaving a gaping, black wound on the Panoptis' back. At the same time, the silver dragon bellowed and collapsed and lay motionless, lifeless, just a few steps before it would have reached the Panoptis.

The Nightson turned to face Alopex, screaming in pain and rage.

"*You dare to give me Death!*"

"I gave you what you wanted you bastard spawn of darkness, and it proved to be too much for you. Curse you to the Pits." Alopex retorted in a cold voice.

Hurting greatly, the Panoptis had brought his hands behind his back and was feeling the wound, the absence of his great eye. All eyes that hadn't yet unmade, snapped open and there were enough of them. They began to close, one by one and Alopex's flesh began to rip open on his chest, his belly, his legs and arms. The king screamed and I wept. Such a pitiful end after such a battle, such determination, such faith and heroism, such sacrifice; all for naught. But the questors weren't yet spent.

Silidora ran towards the monster and she shouted, *"Defender, to me!"* and her magnificent sword, the one that I had thought unmade, appeared at her hands, in its scabbard. It had been mystically hidden and that was the Maiden's last magic and her greatest one. She drew the sword, leapt into the air and slashed with her enchanted blade. I saw the Panoptis' remaining eyes snapping shut in rapid succession but the Maiden's ploy ensured that he didn't have time enough to un-make such power as the sword carried. The head of the Panoptis was half-severed from his body and green blood gushed like a fountain from his neck. Silidora touched the ground and immediately brought the sword into a backwards lunge under her left arm, angled high and with both hands on the hilt. She buried *Defender* into the closed eye of death on the monster's chest and into his black heart.

The Panoptis died and his body fell. I watched mesmerized the flow of blood, which soon slowed to a trickle and then stopped. We had won and we were alive. I was dying but I didn't care; my only regret was that I didn't have strength enough to raise my hand or even to cheer. It was a silent victory, muted by blood, pain and sacrifice.

Silidora came to check on me while Alopex, torn and bloody, went to the still form of the silver dragon and knelt by his head. We both watched the brother-king and we saw his grief melt and his relief shine from his face as tears fell freely. He bent over the head and said something and the dragon began to shrink; the silver of his form rippled and flowed, like water. The dragon assumed the form of Malus and he opened his eyes - he was alive! He was weak and Alopex helped him stand. We went to them and we embraced.

I'd been numb till that moment, numb from pain and from the shock of the battle. The victory, the Panoptis' death, the fact that the horror for me and my people was finally over washed over me like a flood and I cried with tears of joy. Alopex drank from his healing draught, gave

Silidora a few sips and gave me all that remained. A welcome wave of renewal raced through my body as my wounds healed well enough to spare me from death.

"How is this miracle possible?" I asked when I could speak again.

"He was not yet beyond this world." The sylfaea answered me. "His death was held by the eye of death on the Nightson's chest and when I destroyed it, what was done, was undone - the unmade was made again."

"I owe you a debt, Silidora Windwhisper." Malus said.

"You owe me nothing, Dragon, you were my shield and I was your sword. One never owes the other."

"Well said, I'd hate to have to pay off your debts, Malus." Alopex said and grimaced from the pain. "It's over, friends. Let's dress our wounds and be on our way back, away from this evil place."

Malus had been our shield, Silidora had been our sword and Alopex had been our spear, the weapon most blessed, the weapon that gave all mortal races a common identity as Dorians, the People of the Spear. What did that leave for me? It would be presumptuous of me to consider myself equal to those heroes and to give myself a vital role in our victory. I had conquered my fear and I had offered myself as a sacrifice for our victory. That was enough for me.

We made our way back, without delay. We went back, past the bone paintings that held no terror after the destruction of their painter. I filled all the half-moon marks on the walls on the way out.

* * *

Glistenwall Hold.

The joy was evident on the faces of the council elders. Some cried, some only stared at me, struck dumb by the fact that the threat was over and the rest praised our names to the Gods. It was a marked change from the somber and dour faces - accusing even - that I had beheld when I was escorted under guard to the council hall, immediately upon my return. I had returned alone after all. The elders had been afraid that I had abandoned the questors and had fled - a coward still. I was asked to give a full account of the expedition. On our way back from the Panoptis' tunnels, I had asked the questors many questions and so, I had a complete account of our adventure. Therefore, I could give a full account of events to the elders but I didn't. I'd seen and heard too much, through the madness that the Panoptis had afflicted me with. I'd learned things that belonged to the bottom of the blackest pit and I shall never speak of them.

I gave a true account of events but I didn't share the things that pertained to my companions and were private and secret. Those words and deeds I keep in this book only.

"What of the questors, Rathi Breadhands son Harag? Why aren't they here to be greeted as heroes and be feasted as kings?" Chryssa Goldheart asked and the others quieted down and looked at me.

"Alopex Dawnblade, Malus Argent and Silidora Windwhisper do not need to be rewarded for their feats. They asked me to convey their regret that they couldn't return to Glistenwall Hold with me. As you well know, Chryssa Goldheart dal Kendra, they're on a quest of their own. That quest draws them back to the Temple of Glass with urgency. What we can do for them, is to honour their names and spread the tale of the slaying of the consort of the Mother of Madness and so, add to their legend."

Well, the truth was that Alopex wouldn't mind spending the night in a soft bed with his belly full with warm food and strong wine but the Maiden was adamant about making haste back to the temple.

"Our work is not yet done." I said in a loud voice that cut short the chatter of the elders. "We must send a last expedition into the spiral labyrinth and reach its foul heart wherein lies the house that the Panoptis was building for his dark mother."

I paused for emphasis and I made sure that I had the attention of the elders. Chryssa and some others nodded their silent agreement.

"We have offered empty pyres for our dead. It is time to burn their remains and offer to the King of the Underworld the last ashes of our honoured dead." A round of agreements followed my words.

"Who should go on this last expedition, Son of Harag?" Chryssa asked me, as if she could read my mind.

"We all know who must go. There are many among us that live with the shame of their weakness. They should be the ones to do this and no other."

"Will you lead them?" The elder of the Goldheart clan asked me again.

"I will. I have kin for whom I must perform the burial rituals and I have a heirloom to find."

The elders agreed. I had given my account and I had arranged for some redemption for those like myself. It was time to go home to my family. I walked out of the council hall and into the Hold with injuries aplenty, many of which will follow me to the end of my years. I walked out burdened by the weight of dark knowledge, against which only the King of the Gods can be my shield. But I have no regrets, because I walked out with my pride and my heart restored to me.

It was a fair trade.

Epilogue

Year 129 DT, month of Argo.
Earthembar Mountains, the Temple of Glass.

The petraean giant with the skin of gray granite emerged from the cliff-face to stand before the huge obsidian gates. He looked down at the two dorians and the dragon who wore the form of a man of silver. He hadn't expected to see them again. The danaos walked forward. The guardian remembered that he was the king of a small realm somewhere to the north and west and an insolent one at that.

"We meet yet again, guardian of the gate. We return from the quest ordained by the Seeress of Glass as victors. We bring that which she requested. We have seen a Panoptis slain, one who bore twin eyes of death, the consort of the Mother of Madness herself! Open the gates for us and allow Malus Argent to pass them unmolested this time. Do not test our patience or our resolve."

The arrogance of the danaos made the giant's hands clench on the tree-trunk haft of his enormous flail. The chain and flanged ball of bronze could render the danaos into a mere smear on the ground. He should laugh at the danaos king but it wasn't his way to act rashly or carelessly. The Maiden he knew and respected, the dragon he abhorred and feared but the danaos was unknown.

"Do you have that which was demanded?" The giant asked.

The king showed him and the giant's eyes widened and he checked an involuntary gesture to shield his eyes with his arm. The questors had returned as victors indeed. He wouldn't forget Alopex Dawnblade after that day. The guardian of the gate gave the signal for the doors to be opened and then, he retreated into the stone.

Their steps on the cold marble echoed in the vastness of the huge and silent chamber. The walls were decorated with artfully created panels of coloured glass that depicted scenes of everyday life and of giants battling dragons. It was a brightly lit chamber where a kaleidoscope of colours danced about, making one think that he was inside a rainbow. The Seeress of Glass was a giantess of middle age with silvery-gray skin, black hair and stormy gray eyes and she wore an ice-blue peplos. She seemed to be carved from marble as she sat perfectly still on her throne of glass, but her eyes followed the questors and her gaze was intense and expectant. The questors reached the foot of the dais upon which her throne was set and they halted. The dragon in a man's form carried a heavy, copper chest with both hands and he set it down.

"Did you bring what I asked for?" She asked them although she already knew the answer.

"We have." The sylfaea answered.

Alopex opened the lid of the chest. Inside, there was packed snow enveloping a huge eye, filthy with milky-yellow mucus and bloodshot with blue-black veins. She flinched from the malevolence somehow captured in the unseeing gaze of that dead orb. Alopex lifted the chest, ascended the steps to the foot of her throne and placed it on a stand covered with green velvet. He faced the Seeress and said, "Now that we have completed your quest, we demand to hear the oracle we asked for."

She sighed and picked up the frightful thing out of the chest. It was cold and trailed severed muscle fibers and nerves. That dead organ would be her means of seeing inside the realm of a Dark God, where a Demigod lay chained, his soul ravaged. She had hoped to avoid the price of this oracle but the petitioners were before her, conquerors of a Panoptis, saviors of a polis and victors of the quest she had given them. They had already given a king's ransom as offering to the temple. They deserved the oracle.

She gestured and servants brought her a smoking brazier. The herbs that burned there gave off a sweet, heady aroma and she breathed deeply. She could speak prophecy, because she had the strength to become the house for the pneuma of the Titaness Rhea, the Mother of the Olympians and once Queen of the Cosmos. It was rare for dorians to ask the Seeress of Glass for an oracle but neither unheard of, nor forbidden. They were neither her friends, nor her enemies, but against the Dark Gods, they were allies. She would pay a heavy price in order to give them this oracle but she suspected that the cost they'd have to pay would be far greater.

She enacted the ritual and invoked the Godmother to help her on this journey. The eye of the Panoptis became a window into a realm of brutal war, waged only to produce pain, depravity and destruction. And she watched. The sights she had to endure were maddening, they flayed the soul and tormented the spirit. She moaned and swayed on her throne and she spoke prophecy in a voice that changed pitch and volume, a voice that came from the depths of a bottomless pit and was carried to them by the moaning winds of an empty sky.

"I see him, whom you seek and I pity him. The Son of Hecate is lost and alone, a warrior bitterly defeated by his triumph over the Curse of Shadows. He emerged victorious in a war where the enemy was himself but he did not escape his doom. All is not lost however as long as Heroes are willing to rise above the Earth and touch the Sky. If you should be such Heroes, then heed my words..."

The End

The fourth book in The Blades of Dawn series will tell the tale of Glaucos and Prysm who struggle to hold the kingdom together after a difficult winter. The aftermath of the war and the new year bring nothing good to Chalkaea because the Horde of the Black Blood continues to plague the lands of men and an unexpected evil rises to challenge dorian supremacy. It will be another tale of high fantasy set in the Red Years of the Age of Thunder.

Glossary

General

The Cosmos. The universe that was created by the primordial divinities when they brought order unto the formless chaos that existed before the act of creation.

Earth aka the Material or Mortal Plane. A domain composed out of all elements and the body of Gaea. It is given to mortals and banned to immortals by Gaea's decree.

Elemental Planes. Each of the four planes is composed almost entirely by one element.

Aethereal or Spirit Plane. A realm that mirrors the material plane and which is composed out of the fifth element called quintessence.

Astral Plane aka the Realm of Ideal Forms. Therein lie all the names spoken by Gaea when she created the Cosmos.

Dream Plane aka the Dream. Created by Gaea's dreams, it is claimed by the fey.

Mount Olympos. The domain of the Dodecatheon and centre of the Olympian Pantheon.

Dodecatheon. The Twelve Gods who preside over the Olympian Pantheon and the Cosmos.

Olympian. Depending on the context, it may mean one of the first-born Olympians or any divinity that belongs to the Olympian Pantheon.

Pact of the Spear aka the Dorian Pact. The binding agreement between Olympians and the Humans led by Heracles during the Titanomachy which is still in effect.

Dorian. One who has been baptized into the pact of the spear, called dory in the celestial language.

Dorian Nation. The common identity and kinship shared by all dorians.

Olympian Mysteries. A body of lore and ritual offered to any willing dorian who passes certain tests to prove worthy of initiation or of ascension to higher circles. It deepens the bond between mortality and the divine. The highest masters are titled *Hierophants*.

Mount Othrys. Once the abode of Titans and Kronos' seat of power. It is now the domain of the Heavenly Trinity and Uranos' throne.

Heavenly Duality. The Two Gods that preside over all of the immortals and mortals ruled by Uranos. Uranos reigns supreme with the Destroyer (also known as the Nameless Titan) as his right hand.

Compact of Heaven. The binding agreement between the Heavenly

Trinity and their mortal worshippers. In return for lifelong loyalty, obedience and service, mortals are promised an afterlife of hedonistic and materialistic bliss.

Uranian. A worshipper of the Heavenly Trinity who has declared his lifelong loyalty and dedicated his eternal soul to the Compact of Heaven.

Heirless. These are all humans who aren't Dorians. According to the Pact of the Spear, Dorians are the sole inheritors of the Earth, therefore all other men are heirless. However, Uranians are excluded from this group by common convention as they are unequivocally enemies of Dorians whereas the Heirless aren't.

Dragon Calendar (PKD). The acronym stands for the Pangaean Kingdom of Dragons. The first year is considered the beginning of the Age of Catharsis. It is used by the Heirless, including the Uranians and by some sylfaen.

Thunder Calendar (DT). The acronym stands for the Day of Thunder and the first year is considered the beginning of the Age of Thunder. It's the standard dorian calendar.

Soma. A creature's material body.

Nous. The ability to reason and the sum of knowledge possessed only by rational beings.

Pneuma. A creature's spirit, the sum of its experiences during its life.

Psyche. A mortal being's imperishable part which continues to exist after death.

Daimon. The aethereal representation of a living being of the material plane.

The Primordial Divinities

Gaea, aka Mother Earth, the Dreaming Goddess. She committed the first act of creation when she created herself out of primordial chaos. She is *Anagke* or *Need* - forced purpose and direction - and she is also *Desire* - voluntary purpose and direction. Now she sleeps and her dreams have created the Dream Plane.

Uranos, aka Father Sky, the Empty Sky, the Adversary. The husband of Gaea, father of Dragons and Titans, the first King of the Cosmos. After his castration and dethronement, he went into exile. Ages passed and he was forgotten but his need for vengeance and desire for his throne were ever-burning. Eventually he returned and brought with him the Dark Host to wage war upon the Cosmos. Now he is the Adversary.

Tartaros. He is the primordial chaos, outside the rules of creation, a force unto himself. His only need is the end of order and his only desire is the dissolution of the Cosmos into the primordial chaos that preceded it. He lies punished in the abyssal depths in eternal stasis and his body is pitted with pits carved out of his flesh by fiends and by the dark gods.

Nyx. She is the darkness, the lower half of the circle. She resides in Gaea's Dream with her husband Helios in an eternal twilight.

Helios. He is the light, the upper half of the circle but he is dimmed by his regrets over failing to protect his wife from Tartaros.

The Immortals

Dragons, aka the Firstborn. The first race birthed by the union of Gaea and Uranos. They were made in the image of their father.

Titans. The second race birthed by the union of Gaea and Uranos. They were made in the image of their mother.

Olympians. The six sons and daughters of King Kronos and Queen Rhea - presently the rulers of the Cosmos. The title is more broadly applied to the Dodecatheon as well as to all divinities that belong to the Olympian Pantheon.

Dark Host, aka the Dark Gods. The children of Tartaros and Nyx that allied with Uranos and returned with him to make war upon all the creatures of creation. They reside in the Pits of Tartaros.

Echidna, aka the Mother of Monsters. A daughter of Gaea, she has given birth to many creatures terrible and foul and she is the enemy of olympians and dorians.

Typhon, aka the Destroyer. A son of Gaea and Echidna's husband. He's also an enemy of the Olympians and their dorian worshippers and one of the most terrible adversaries that Zeus had to contend with during the Titanomachy.

Heracles. Born a demigod, he was instrumental in the victory of the Olympians over the Titans in the Titanomachy and responsible for the forging of the pact of the spear. He was granted immortality by his father, Zeus.

The Fey. A diverse collection of beings that includes all the nymphs (naiads, nereids, dryads, auras and more) as well as satyrs, gnomes, pixies, sprites and others. Beings of whimsy, passion and desire who reject anagke and morality.

The Beast Lords. The perfect form of each animal race, embodied in one individual who is a rational being and can usually assume a human form. A being of two worlds, capable of intellectual pursuit, spiritual awareness and naked savagery.

The Moirae

Three daughters of Nyx and Helios, they became the embodiment of *Anagke* after Gaea divested herself of this aspect. After guiding her son to castrate her husband, the Mother of All wished no more to be the Cosmos' Need and so gifted this aspect to the Moirae. The sisters took upon themselves the roles of architects of Fate and overseers of Destiny. Kronos ignored them during his reign but Zeus empowered them and accepted them as an integral part of his Olympian cosmic order. The relationship between the Moirae and the Olympians is complex but one thing is clear; Zeus does not rule them. They are the Fates as much of immortals as they are of mortals.

Clotho. The youngest sister, she forever spins and weaves the destiny of mortals and marvels at each thread. New life never ceases to fill her with wonder.

Lachesis. The middle sister, she forever measures the thread of each mortal and apportions to him what is his due. She is moved by forced purpose in every gesture or word, as much the stern master of a mortal life as its loyal servant.

Atropos. The elder sister, she is ever ready to cut a thread with her shears, whether mortal or immortal. Ultimate arbiter of life or death, her hands move as much by her own conscience and judgement as by cosmic direction.

The Elder Races

Gigas [gigantes (pl.)], aka Primordial Giants. The first race born by Gaea after the sundering of her marriage with Uranos. Their father was the Serpent Lord and they have always been enemies of Dragons. They fought with the Titans in the Titanomachy and were vanquished by the Olympians.

Giants. The offspring of Gigantes that were gaean in form. A diverse race that was once proud but is now subservient to dorians - in spirit if not always in practice - by Olympian decree.

Elder Beasts. All beings and races created during the first three mythic ages by either Gaea or Echidna that are bestial in form. Many of them are chimeric beings and most of them are rational but not all. The most well-known are the Chimaera, the Manticore, the Sphinx and the Gryphon.

The Human Races

These are the races that share the gaean form, rationality and a common bond that transcends the ages. With one exception, mating between individuals of different human races will produce a child that shares the mother's race.

Danaos [danae (fem.), danaoi (pl.), danaan (adj.)]. A race of people that were created by the dragons out of clay, water and breath and were given a place in the world by the lonely sylfaen.

Sylfos [sylfaea (fem.), sylfaen (pl.), sylfan (adj.)] aka the Titan-born. Born along with the goddess Aphrodite out of Uranos' sperm and blood that fell in the sea after his castration. Time had not yet began which is why they are ageless although they are mortal. They are also considered an Elder Race.

Chalyvos [chalyvaea (fem.), chalyvoi (pl.), chalyvan (adj.)]. Crafted in Hephaestos' forge and granted the breath of life by Queen Hera, they are a stout race but short and unlovely to the eye, like their creator. The term *Dwarf* is widely used in a derogatory fashion.

Centaur [centaura (fem.), centaurs (pl.), centauran (adj.)]. A proud race with a hybrid form of horse and human. The first centaurs were the children of the Oceanid Nymph Nephele and the human king Ixion. Poseidon favoured this race and so the Centaurs thrived but remained ever wild.

Alfhos [alfhaea (fem.), alfhaen (pl.), alfhan(adj.)]. The products of the union between danaoi and sylfaen, a union blessed by Aphrodite, the Goddess of Love.

Spartos [sparte (fem.), spartoi (pl.), spartan (adj.)]. A very rare race that came into being when Cadmos sowed a True Dragon's teeth while bestowed with the grace of both Ares and Athena and then ploughed the earth. Tall and strong, armed and armoured warriors sprung from the earth, possessing conscience, reason, memory of history and knowledge of their own worth.

The Dark Races

Darkspawn, aka Darkin. The mortal races fashioned by the Dark Gods in their image by corrupting the flesh and minds of humans and animals. Their darksouls are fragments of broken human souls. They form diverse tribes that are a blight upon the world and humanity. Their common traits are brutality and stupidity, rudimentary capacity for crafts and inability to produce art. Their defining trait is the dark gift of *Yikimcholg*. Some of the more prominent races are,

Oroks. The most reviled dark race. The name is common in all languages.

Goblins or Kucuk (pitspeak). They are puny, stupid and cowardly but their numbers are uncountable.

Wolfgoblins or Wargchuk (pitspeak). When goblins bond with darkwolves, they become smarter and more capable.

Darkwolves or Wargs (pitspeak). Mutated wolves of varying size. They commonly bond with goblins and allow them as riders.

Beastmen or Arpaks (pitspeak). Bestial hybrids of man and animal.

Chaosmen, Chaosbeasts or Trollvores (pitspeak). Darkin or humans mutated by dark magic. No two are alike and they're greatly feared.

Death-Feast or Yikimcholg (pitspeak). Acts of defilement or destruction of the natural world and the murder of humans, animals and other beings of Creation, provide sustenance to darkspawn. The burning of trees, the pollution of rivers, the torture and killing of men and animals, the ruination of the works of men - all of these acts sustain the darkspawn who participate and so, large numbers of darkin can survive without food or water indefinitely as long as they commit such depraved acts.

The Devils, aka Fiends, Nightsons, Darkdaughters

They are progeny of the Dark Gods and they are uniformly loathsome in body, mind and spirit. They can be mortal or immortal, a singular being or a multitude. They are always corrupters and destroyers, beings of infinite sins and no virtues, inimical to Creation.

Mysticism

Magic. The capacity for the manipulation of the mind, matter and the elements. Manipulation of the soul and the creation or sustenance of life are possible only with divine providence.

Magganea, aka Dark Magic. The capacity for the dissolution of creation and the ability to manipulate the primordial force of chaos.

Orphic Secrets. The mystical methodology and body of lore compiled by the legendary Orpheas in a previous mythic age, in order to codify the secrets of mysticism and teach the discipline required for the safe use of magic by mortals.

Mystic. A practitioner of the mystical arts or crafts according to the Orphic Secrets. It is an umbrella term for the followers of the various disciplines that include the Magi, Theurgoi, Minstrels, Spellweavers,

Thaumatourgoi, Sorcerers, Technarchs, Necromancers and Hieromystics.

Spellcaster. A general and common term for a practitioner of magic. Proper use of the term, observed by philosophers and orphic loremasters, describes a practitioner of magic outside the bounds of the Orphic Secrets.

Dark Mystic. A term used by dorians to describe spellcasters of the dark races.

Hieros [hiere (fem.), hieroi (pl.), hiero (adj.)]. A blessed dorian who has the ability to channel divine power so as to heal injury and disease. Hieroi are not necessarily mystics.

Spell. A unique instance of the use of magic. It strictly describes an instance of magic-use outside Orphism but commonly it also applies to orphic magic.

Praxis [praxes (pl.)]. It is the totality of casting a spell but it is also commonly used to describe each stage of spellcasting. The meaning depends on context. It applies strictly to orphic magic.

Archetype, aka Ideal Form. The foundation of every spell, found in the astral plane as the ideal spiritual representation of a named object or being.

Schema [schemata (pl.)]. The construct of the spell in the aethereal plane, built upon its archetypal foundation and filled with quintessence.

Pragma [pragmata (pl.)]. A free-standing mystical construct.

Ephemeron. An item invested with magic which is either consumable or of limited duration.

Hemiteles. An item that holds a limited amount of magic but which can be refilled.

Hermetic. An item of limitless magical power (in source, not in scope).

Life in the Dorian World

Society is divided between the common men, the aristocracy, the archons and the king. *Archon* is the common title of a ruler who's subservient to a king, no matter the actual title. A king must be approved by both men and Zeus in order to rule. A city's proper name is *Polis*. Units of measurement is the *kilogram* and *ton* for weight and the *metre* and *kilometre* for distance. A *stadio* or *stadion* is an intermediate unit equal to 200 metres.

Houses are made of timber, clay bricks and stone and the roofs are sloping and covered with ceramic tiles. The wealthy houses have two stories and the interior has a central courtyard. Traditionally, an entire family of three generations lives in a house together. In such a case, men and women have their own spaces - the *Andron* is for the men and the *Gynaikon* is for the women. Glass panes are for the wealthy and wooden shutters cover the windows.

The house of healing is called *Asclepeion* and it's also considered a temple to the God of Healing, Asclepeios. Temples are also houses of healing. The healer is called *Therapon*. Marriage is a sacred union between man and woman. *Philosopher* is the title of wise men and they are scientists and teachers. A formal school is called *Academy* and only the largest and most prominent cities have one. Children are schooled by their parents, by priests who are so inclined or by hired philosophers if their parents are wealthy or if they live near an academy. All children learn to read and write and they also learn music and arithmetic. All boys are required to exercise from a young age.

A *Kitharodos* is a common musician and this name derives from the kithara, a stringed instrument considered fit only for an audience of commoners. A *Minstrel* is a learned musician who sings well, plays many instruments and is also a dancer. A *Rhapsodos* is the most re-vered musician, a title reserved for the paragons of this craft. This title also applies to the master mystic of an army.

Sports and athletic competitions are an important part of the dorian world. Every kingdom hosts annual games where athletes compete and winners gain glory.

War in the Dorian World

War is a vital part of life and all men are expected to possess at least a spear and a sling and know how to use them. The usual roles of sol-diers are,

Hoplite. The most well-trained and heavily armed soldier, member of a phalanx. Armed with hoplitic spear and hoplon. Chalyvoi as a rule cannot fight alongside the taller races as hoplites.

Infantry. All other footmen, armed and armoured in any manner but trained adequately as regular troops able to hold formation and maneuver as a unit.

Peltast. Lightly armoured and armed with sling and javelin. Young and swift runners, they are irregular troops.

Archer. Lightly armoured and armed with any type of bow. Chalyvoi use the crossbow instead because of their short stature. They are irregular troops.

Cavalier. Troops mounted on horses. There is a great variety of units with *Knights* being the most heavily armed and armoured and the most well-trained.

The most common army unit is the *Company* of 200 to 400 men. it's subdivided into two *Demi-Companies* (each is half the company), *Sworn Squads* (25 men) and *Decarchies* (10 men). In large armies, a *Regiment* is comprised of 2 or 3 companies and a *Taxiarchy* is comprised of 2 or 3 regiments. The most revered army unit is the *Phalanx*, a unit of any size (usually of company size) composed exclusively by hoplites. The term *Battalion* is reserved for special forces that are not set in size or composition. The officer titles are,

Strategos. Commands the army.

Taxiarchos, aka Taxiarch. Commands a taxiarchy.

Colonel. Commands a regiment.

Captain. Commands a company.

The term *Sergeant* is in general use for the three lower ranks,

Arch-Sergeant. Commands a demi-company.

Sworn Sergeant. Commands a sworn squad.

Decarch. Commands a decarchy.

The most common arms are the hoplitic spear (a heavy and long spear for use in the phalanx), the common spear, the xiphos (a short sword), the kopis (an inwards curving sword), the club, the sling and the short bow. Sylfaen favour the leafblade (a longer sword), chalyvoi favour the warhammer, battleaxe and crossbow and centaurs favour the lance, warclub and long bow. The metal parts of weapons are made of bronze or steel.

The most common armours are the bronze chestplate and leg greaves, the metal-studded, leather wings for the groin and upper legs, the bronze or steel helmet and the linothorax - a chestpiece made of linen and other materials in layers. The shield is the most important piece of an infantryman's armaments and it is round except for the chalyvan ones that are square. The most revered piece of a soldier's arms is the *Hoplon*, the large, round shield used by hoplites.

Seasons, Months and Time in the Dorian World

The seasonal cycle is mandated by the Gods, especially by Demeter. Winter begins when her daughter, Persephone descends to the Underworld and represents her mother's grief and disapproval. Spring begins when the Daughter returns to Olympos and her mother rejoices. The cycles of day and night have 12 hours each, to honour the Dodecatheon in everyday life. Noon and Midnight are the 6th hour of each cycle. The actual duration of each hour lengthens or shortens according to the season. Time is kept with sundials during the day and with water clocks called *Clepsydrai* (singular *Clepsydra*) during the night or on cloudy days. Even so, people cannot actually tell what time it is with accuracy in everyday life so when they speak of hours, it's a generality.

The year has 12 months and 360 days and nights. Each month is named after the constellation that is prominent at the sky during that month. The odd months have 28 days while the even months have 29 days. The *Noumenia* - the first day of each month - is a holy day devoted to one of the Twelve Olympians. Each month is divided into 7-day weeks. Each day is named and the Sun Day, the first of each week, is a day of rest. The 29th day bears no name or rather it bears a secret name known only to wise astronomers and adepts of the Orphic Secrets.

The 18 days that belong to no month, are organized in six triads which are interjected in the calendar right after each pair of an odd and an even month. Each triad is devoted to one of the Firstborn Olympians. The new year begins at the Spring season. Demeter's Triad heralds the new year, before the month of the Eagle.

There are two moons, Selene, the silver moon and Luna, the scarlet moon. The silver moon is the largest and follows a steady cycle of 28 days. It is a symbol of Artemis and she is worshipped by women and children on the nights of the full moon. The scarlet moon is smaller and governed by rules that the mortal mind cannot easily grasp. It is a symbol of Hecate and the phases it goes through are neither regular nor predictable. Mystics study the scarlet moon and try to predict its phases and understand its cycle because it often has a bearing on spells and works of magic. Mystical pathways in particular are easier or more difficult to find and walk, depending on the scarlet moon's phase. Luna's only predictable phases are the night of the full moon on Hecate's noumenia and the fact that it's visible in the sky in the 29th day of each even month.

The natural cycle and the average temperature is the same at any location of Gaea. Only the altitude of tall mountains, the vast sea deeps and the dark depths under the earth differ in climate and temperature.

The most common calendar in Dorian realms measures the passing of years from the Day of Thunder. It was the day that marked the return of Zeus and the Olympians to lordship over the Cosmos after the dethronement of Dragons. This measure of time is marked with the letters 'DT'. Heirless and some among the long-lived sylfaen continue to measure time since the founding of the Pangaean Kingdom of Dragons which marked the beginning of the previous age, the Age of Katharsis. This measure of time is marked with 'PKD'. All calendars begin with year one, not zero.

There are numerous constellations in the sky and they wheel around the North Star throughout the year. Twelve of them are the most prominent and each one shines brightest in a cycle that conforms to the cycle of months. These constellations are said to bestow personality or metaphysical traits upon newbons born under their influence.

Spring Season

Demeter's Triad (new year), **Eagle** (28 Days, Zeus' Noumenia), **Argo** (29 Days, Hephaestos' Noumenia), *Poseidon's Triad*, **Orion** (28 Days, Artemis' Noumenia).

Summer Season

Heracles (29 Days, Athena's Noumenia), *Hestia's Triad*, **Chiron** (28 Days, Apollon's Noumenia), **Dolphin** (29 Days, Poseidon's Noumenia).

Autumn Season

Hera's Triad, **Bootes** (28 Days, Demeter's Noumenia), **Stephanos** (29 Days, Hera's Noumenia), *Zeus' Triad*, **Leon** (28 Days, Ares' Noumenia).

Winter Season

Andromeda (29 Days, Aphrodite's Noumenia), *Hades' Triad*, **Kerberos** (28 Days, Hermes' Noumenia), **Lyra** (29 Days, Hecate's Noumenia).

The Selenean Weeks

First week of the First Half-Moon also known as *Moonbow Week*.
Second week of the Full Moon also known as *Moonshield Week*.
Third week of the Last Half-Moon also known as *Bloodsickle Week*.
Fourth week of the New Moon also known as *Starbright Week*.

The Seven Weekdays

First, Sun Day also known as *Sunday*.
Second, Moon Day also known as *Moonday*.
Third , Zeus Day also known as *Kingsday*.
Fourth, Hera's Day also known as *Queensday*.

Fifth, Hades' Day also known as *Greyday*.

Sixth, Poseidon's Day also known as *Seaday*.

Seventh, Gaea's Day also known as *Earthday*.

The Constellations

Golden Eagle. Month of the *Eagle*. The eagle - also called Thunderbird - is favoured by Zeus. It's the herald of rain and the bringer of omens from the King of the Gods.

The Hero's Ship. Month of *Argo*. The ship of heroes, crafted by Hephaestos and given as a gift to Jason by Athena. Argo's maidenhead had the power of speech and advised Jason.

Princess Andromeda. Month of *Andromeda*. She was renowned for her beauty and betrayed by her mother. She was saved by the hero Perseus and she was the great grandmother of Heracles.

The Stalwart Hunter. Month of *Orion*. A son of Poseidon, Orion was a skilled and renowned hunter. Artemis came to love him but before they could consummate their love, her brother, Apollon, challenged Orion in an archery duel. Orion accepted but lost the contest and his life. Hera placed Orion's soul as a constellation in the heavens to soften Artemis' sorrow.

Great Heracles. Month of *Heracles*. The most prominent mortal son of Zeus. His mother was the mortal woman Alcmene. He is the greatest hero of the Dorian Nation and the forger of the Pact of the Spear between mortals and Gods during the Titanomachy. He gained immortality and a place in Olympos.

The Wise Centaur. Month of *Chiron*. He was a son of Kronos and recognized far and wide for his wisdom. He taught many heroes and some of the gods and demigods. Eventually, he divested himself of his immortality and was placed among the stars.

The Sacred Dolphin. Month of the *Dolphin*. The loyal and gentle companion of Poseidon and the one that persuaded the nymph Amphitrite to wed the God of the Sea. It is ever a friend to sailors and companion of all sea dwellers.

The Ploughman. Month of *Bootes*. He was the inventor of the wagon and the plough. He was placed among the stars by his mother, Demeter.

Corona or the Crown. Month of *Stephanos*. The crown of rulership worn by Zeus and all mortal kings who rule under the auspices of the King of the Gods.

Leon or Lion. Month of *Leon*. The original Lion Lord was favoured by Ares and fought with him in the Titanomachy. He fell in battle and was placed among the stars in recognition of his supremacy as King of Beasts.

Kerberos. Month of *Kerberos*. The terrible dog of Hades with three heads and a snake-tail. It is the guardian of the gate to the Underworld.

Lyra or Lyre. Month of *Lyra*. A beloved musical instrument and one of the oldest. Orpheas, the codifier of all mystical secrets, practiced mysticism through music and his chosen instrument was the lyre.